T0107292

Too Much Rain

The Flood of the Century

L. Louis Marchino

iUniverse, Inc.
New York   Bloomington

Too Much Rain
The Flood of the Century

iUniverse books may be ordered through booksellers or by contacting:

iUniverse
1663 Liberty Drive
Bloomington, IN 47403
www.iuniverse.com
1-800-Authors (1-800-288-4677)

Because of the dynamic nature of the Internet, any Web addresses or links contained in this book may have changed since publication and may no longer be valid. The views expressed in this work are solely those of the author and do not necessarily reflect the views of the publisher, and the publisher hereby disclaims any responsibility for them.

ISBN: 978-1-4401-4387-8 (sc)
ISBN: 978-1-4401-4389-2 (cloth)
ISBN: 978-1-4401-4388-5 (ebk)

Printed in the United States of America

iUniverse rev. date: 5/18/2009

Thanks to Larry

Prologue

"There is a large high pressure system over Lake Ontario and a large high pressure system over Raleigh North Carolina. These two systems have been bringing beautiful weather to the Eastern seaboard. They have been hanging there for the last eight days, effectively blocking the huge low-pressure system that is bringing so much misery and destruction to the entire Midwest. This monster low is feeding on an abundance of moisture that is streaming steadily up from the Gulf of Mexico and also from the Pacific Ocean."

That was how the weather forecast started on that Saturday morning the 12th day of June.

The announcer continued, "This is unprecedented, some locations have reported as much as an inch per hour, for a period of 4, 5, or as much as 6 hours at a time. Not many areas can handle that much rain, even in a dry season, without some flooding. This is occurring intermittently, sometimes frequently, over southern South Dakota, southern Minnesota, southwestern Wisconsin, Nebraska, Iowa, Illinois, Missouri and parts of Arkansas and southern Indiana.

"It's safe to say that there is serious flooding somewhere in all of these areas. There are many reports of roads and bridges that have been washed out. It will be months before the transportation systems in these areas can return to normal. The cost of the cleanup and restoration of these communities will be astronomical.

L. Louis Marchino

"The forecast sounds like a broken record, more of the same."

Contents

The Flood Of The Century

Chapter 1

Friday Morning

Roy Johnson was awakened by the sudden sound of wind driven raindrops beating hard against the bedroom window, immediately followed by a loud crash of thunder. It was just a few minutes before six o-clock, the time he usually got up to go to work. He probably would have overslept this morning. He had been unsettled and disturbed last night thinking about all that was ahead of him. He had told Hank two weeks ago that this Thursday, June10, would be his last day on the job. Now today was Friday. He had much to do.

From the time he was a kid in grade school he had been around heavy machinery and construction equipment. His father Joe Johnson had owned the Johnson Construction Company, so Roy was exposed to the big machines frequently even as a small child.

Before Roy was born Joe brought Hank Wells in as a junior partner. At first Joe owned 65 percent and Hank owned 35 percent of the business. Hank was the first man Joe had hired when he started the business, but they worked as equals and Roy grew up with both of them. Hank loved him as his own son and Roy was as apt to be in the cab of one of those monster machines with Hank as he was with his father. They often let him take the controls for a while. By the time he was 13 and a freshman in high school he could handle the basic elementary maneuvers of any of the machines, always under the close supervision of his dad or Hank. His understanding of the capabilities and limits of the machines and his well-coordinated, accurate touch on the controls made him an "expert without credentials" by the time he was 15.

Roy had talked to Hank a month ago when he had put their, now his, home in the hands of a realtor. She had promised a quick sale because of the location and the very reasonable price Roy was asking.

All this was going through his mind as he sat on the edge of his bed. This would be the last night he would spend at Mrs. Olson's boarding house.

He dressed quickly in a flannel shirt, one of his better pairs of jeans, and his best cowboy boots. The shirt was a red plaid, his favorite, and one that his wife Mary Ann had gotten for him last Christmas. He only wore it on special occasions.

Today was a momentous occasion!

He would leave Hank and the only job he had ever known. At 23, he had been a heavy equipment operator almost 8 years. He still loved it but he had to leave Bentlyville. The pain was too great.

When he was a kid Hank had always let him hang around the office and the shop where the mechanics and operators worked to keep the big machines humming.

At first some of the mechanics and operators resented Roy's presence and his incessant questioning. They soon realized, however, that Roy was a quick study and a knowledgeable and willing helper. If they asked him to hand them a half-inch drive Torque wrench or a three quarter inch Ratchet or a myriad of other tools, he almost always came up with the right tool and the right size.

He also learned the hand signals that backhoe, dragline, and crane operators relied on when working in the blind. Roy loved the roar of the huge engines that powered those great machines and the smell of the diesel fumes that was always present. He enjoyed and was part of the good-natured camaraderie of the operators when they climbed down from those lofty cabs.

When he reached age 16 and obtained a driver's license, Hank put him on the payroll as a steady employee except when he was in school. He played on the high school baseball team and on the high school basketball team. Hank and Joe and Helen attended almost every game. Roy's Mother Helen never missed a game. Joe and Hank each had to miss two baseball games in his whole high school career.

Roy's 23-year-old half sister, Ellie, came as often as she could. Roy was a natural athlete and played two years on the college baseball team. In his second year as first-string third base man he had the second highest batting average on the team.

After two years of college he left with an A.S. degree in diesel mechanics and went home to work full time as a mechanic or an operator for Hank.

Joe had retired when Roy was still in high school, so Hank was now the owner of Johnson Construction Company.

Shortly after Roy came home from college, Hank, on Joe's advice, bid on a very large construction job in western Pennsylvania. Hank asked Joe to go with him to Pennsylvania to see the prospective job. It looked good to both of them and Hank got the contract.

It took several weeks to arrange all of the details. It was going to take more and in some cases larger equipment than Johnson Construction Company had so Hank sold, leased, and traded some of his old machines and bought some new equipment to be delivered to the new jobsite.

In mid September Hank and Roy and six other long time and trusted employees all with wives, and some with wives and small children, left for Bentlyville, Pennsylvania.

And now Roy would leave this job. This life that he and Mary Ann had lived was gone. Forever.

The life that he and Mary Ann had created was also gone. Forever.

For a moment emotion overwhelmed him. He drew a deep breath and a sob choked in his throat. He stayed that way for a moment. His breath did not come easy. Gradually the pain subsided. He wiped his eyes on a clean handkerchief that had lain in a drawer near some of Mary Ann's things.

Her scent was there.

And again the powerful emotion grasped him; it was as if someone had grabbed him by the throat. He staggered back to the bed and sat down with his face in his hands and sobbed openly for a few minutes, holding the handkerchief tightly to his face.

He hadn't broken down like this but once since the funeral. That was when he had packed Mary Ann's things to give to the Salvation Army, and Dorothy Ann's little things to go to the orphanage.

He had to make himself stop thinking about these things. It was over. Finished. It could never be that way again.

Eventually, rationality overcame the strong emotions that had taken control of him. He put the handkerchief in the laundry bag with a few other things that Mrs. Olson was going to wash and send to him at his father's place in Kansas. Then he went to the bathroom and washed his face and combed his hair for the second time. He was beginning to feel ready to meet the world again.

He had to go to the Post Office to tell them where to forward his mail. He had go to the bank to tell them his father's address and to be prepared to transfer his account to another bank.

Roy's banking and savings accounts were quite large. They had all been joint accounts but Roy, as recently as two months ago, had them all put in his name only. His checking account held over one thousand dollars. He had a little over five hundred dollars in cash in his wallet, plus two credit cards, which he seldom used.

Barring trouble of some kind the five hundred in his wallet should be more than enough to cover travel expenses for two or three days. And a phone call would get enough money transferred from one of his two savings accounts to his checking account to do about anything he could foresee.

Money would not be a problem.

He left the rooming house and made his rounds taking care of the details and saying good-bye to a few special friends.

When he had taken care of these incidentals, he made one more stop to say good-bye to Hank.

Hank came to meet him as soon as he pulled into the parking lot.

Hank said, "Roy, you have always been like a son to me. It just won't seem right without you here. I sure hope you won't stay away too long."

Roy looked down at his boots and replied, " I know, Hank, one way I don't want to leave, but I have to. I just have to get away from this town. There are too many bad memories here."

Hank said, "I know, Roy, I understand, but you've been my right hand man for so long I'm not sure how I'll handle it."

" Hank, if I wasn't sure Clarence could handle my job I wouldn't leave until he could. You've got a good crew here and they'll do right by you."

After a few more regretful good byes and good lucks Roy drove out of the parking lot without looking back.

He drove back to Mrs. Olson's rooming house and picked up the last of his belongings and carried them out to the pickup.

As he was stowing some small items behind and under the seat, Mrs. Olson came out with a package and she said,

"I'll put this in the cooler, Roy." Roy was preoccupied with what he was doing and he really didn't hear what she said as she opened the lid on the large cooler in the truck bed and laid the package in the bottom of the nearly empty cooler.

Roy said, "Thanks, Mrs. Olson," and went ahead with the task at hand. When he was finished he backed out of the cab of the pickup, and Mrs. Olson, who had been watching sadly, said,

"You will write or call won't you, Roy?" Roy gave her a little hug and said,

"I sure will, Mrs. Olson. You've really been nice to me and I won't forget it."

She wiped at a tear that spilled down her wrinkled cheek and as Roy climbed into the cab she said, "I'll pray for you, Roy."

Roy drove away knowing he was leaving some true friends.

He had one more stop to make; he turned on to his old street. Just down the block he pulled in to a familiar driveway.

The real estate sign was gone and the name on the mailbox had been painted over. There were no curtains in the windows.

"But!" Roy wanted to scream, ***"This Was Mine!"*** He slowly backed down the driveway. He turned to go back the way he had come, but he stopped, holding back the tears, and looked once more at the still familiar sight.

Then he slowly drove down the street.

Chapter 2

Roy's Father

Joe Johnson started the Johnson Construction Company when he was 41 years old. He started very small. His only equipment was a small bulldozer and a backhoe. He did everything himself, the bidding, the contracting, the paper work, the collecting, and when one of the machines started up, Joe was at the controls.

Joe handled everything himself for about a year, and then his wife Virginia started helping with the office work. She worked in the office right through her pregnancy.

Joe was 43 and Virginia was 39 when their only child Ellen or soon to become Ellie was born.

Virginia continued to work in the office after Ellie was born and everything ran smoothly.

When Ellie was three Virginia started having health problems. Joe tried to keep up the office work when she did not feel well enough to come in to the office. But it soon proved to be more than Joe could handle and still keep the machines running.

Helen Kelly was the first applicant to answer the ad for an office manager that Joe had posted on the bulletin board at the local family owned restaurant. Helen was a widow with general office work and book keeping experience. She went to work the next day.

Helen was in her mid thirties, very pleasant and efficient. She handled the office routine as if she had always run a construction company. Joe found her to be invaluable. It freed him up to spend more time with Virginia and Ellie and also to keep the work going.

During this time Joe's business was booming. He had hired Hank sometime right after Ellie was born, and he had talked to Hank several times about coming in as a partner. Hank wanted to be a partner, but he was always afraid to invest his savings. Finally, Joe talked him into it. He became a junior partner. They were good friends and worked well together.

When Ellie was 5, Virginia was diagnosed with a devastating, quick growing breast cancer. The surgeons found the cancer too far advanced. It had invaded other organs.

It was incurable.

When Ellie's mother became too sick to look after her, Helen suggested, "Mr. Johnson, you could bring Ellie to the office during the day, and she could stay with me. I'm sure we would get along fine."

The suggestion was a Godsend to Joe. He was at his wit's end. The doctors had told Joe that his wife's illness was terminal and the time was short.

She died 4 weeks before Ellie's 6th birthday.

After his wife's death, Joe was too devastated to be much help, so Hank was initiated into the business suddenly and without fanfare. He and Helen ran things smoothly and without any insurmountable problems

Joe tried to take care of little Ellie but there were so many times he just felt totally inadequate and unable to cope with the situation.

Again Helen came to the rescue.

It was time for Ellie to start school.

Joe asked Helen to take her to school and get her enrolled and get her school clothes and supplies.

Helen handled those chores with her usual efficiency. She and Ellie got along great. This was a great relief to Joe.

There were days when Ellie would become sad and morose and would cry, but somehow Helen would always know how to comfort her. She would hold Ellie and stroke her long dark hair while talking soothingly and soon Ellie would be her vibrant, energetic self again.

Joe noted these incidents with awe and great appreciation of Helen's uncanny ability to always, immediately, come up with the appropriate response to a problem.

It was two or three months later that he started noticing her as a woman. He liked her dark hair and eyes that always seemed to be smiling. She had a pretty face with a wide mouth and full lips. He never saw her without just a trace of lipstick. He had never allowed himself to admire her figure but now he realized it was quite admirable, with high, full, breasts, a slim waist, seductively flared hips, and long legs. She was nearly as tall as Joe's 5' 10" if she wore heels, which she seldom did, but her most endearing characteristic was her personality, a confident smile, a bright, cheerful outlook, a quick wit, and unquestionable honesty.

The first week after the funeral, Helen saw Joe struggling to cope with everything and saw Ellie's confusion. It pained her to see the little girl trying to understand all that had happened in the past few weeks. Her heart went out to both of them.

Helen again suggested, "Mr. Johnson, if you'd like, I could see Ellie off to school in the morning and pick her up in the evening. She could stay at my house until you close the office each evening and then you could pick her up at my house on your way home."

Joe said, "Helen, I know that will be best for Ellie, and it will certainly take a load off of my mind, if it's not to much to ask of you."

Helen said, "Not at all, Mr. Johnson, I can have the office work under control by the time school is out and I'll be glad to have Ellie's company in the afternoon."

So that was settled and the routine suited Ellie just fine. But soon, Ellie asked her father if she could stay over at Helen's. After the third time Ellie pleaded with Joe to stay over, Joe discussed it with Helen.

Helen convincingly assured Joe that she would enjoy Ellie's presence in her house day or night.

It was true. She and Ellie had formed a close relationship, almost like sisters, or Mother and daughter?

Joe thought, "This Helen is a truly remarkable woman." He could see Ellie's love for Helen.

After two weeks of this arrangement Joe asked Helen and Ellie to go with him to the local restaurant for supper.

They had an enjoyable evening. They listened to Ellie's stories from school and they talked about how well Hank was doing with the road job. Ellie told Joe how Helen let her help with the dishes, and Helen was teaching her how to crochet! She just beamed as she told Joe about these things. Joe was proud of Ellie and very grateful to Helen. He could see that Helen was as proud of Ellie as he was.

More and more frequently they had their evening meal together. Ellie seemed to be happiest during those evenings, and Joe and Helen found that they also enjoyed each other's company. At Joe's request, Helen stopped calling him, Mr. Johnson. They found it easy to all be together.

In all their time working together there had never been any physical contact between them except a time or two in the office when they accidentally bumped into one another. It had never been anything but a purely platonic relationship.

One evening at the restaurant Joe was very concerned about a large contract he was considering signing.

If he did undertake the job, he would probably have to buy or lease another bulldozer and a huge crane. This would require financing. He sat mulling over his options with a worried look on his face.

Helen reached over and softly laid her hand on his hand. "Joe," she said, " I checked over the books this afternoon. If you want to sign that contract, your finances are solid and you have a good reserve. I studied the contract. It gives you lots of leeway on time to finish."

Joe hardly heard what she said. The electricity of her touch stirred him more than he thought possible. Her hand was still on his. He looked at it. Then with a deliberate motion he took his other hand and covered her hand and looked into her eyes.

As he looked into her eyes, Joe felt a sudden fullness in his chest and the words welled up in his throat. The truths he had not known were there, suddenly came out.

He said, "Helen, you are the most important person in my life. Please don't ever leave me." He now held her hand in both of his and his grip tightened. "I need you in every way," he said.

Helen's gaze was as unwavering as Joe's as she said, "I think I feel the same way, Joe. I'm not thinking about leaving."

Ellie had been watching intently as a waitress balancing a huge tray of food carried it carefully between the tables and served the six businessmen at a large table across the room. Ellie was impressed. She was so preoccupied watching the waitress that she missed the exchange between Joe and Helen, but just caught the last words that Helen had said, "about leaving".

" Oh, Helen, please don't go away." She grabbed Helen's right hand with both of hers. (Joe still held her left) Helen gently slid her left hand from Joe's grasp and encircling Ellie with both arms, she soothingly said.

"Don't worry, honey. I'm going to stay right here."

Ellie looked up, her eyes brimming with tears that were about ready to fall and smiled through the tears and said, "Oh, I'm so glad, Helen. I want you to always be here."

Helen looked up and her eyes met Joe's across the table and from that moment it was a forgone conclusion, a complete understanding. There would be a wedding.

When the dessert was served, Joe said, again looking into Helen's soft brown eyes,

"Helen, if you are consenting and don't think I'm too old for you, do you think it would be appropriate to set a date?"

"Joe," she said, understanding perfectly, "I think I already have one and I don't think 50 is old."

That night Joe stayed over at Helen's house. This pleased Ellie greatly.

Helen took over all the details, which was exactly what Joe wanted her to do. The wedding would be June 27.

This would be just a little over 11 months since the death of Joe's wife.

The days went swiftly by. Almost every night they spent together, some nights at Joe's house and some nights at Helen's. Of course the tongues had been wagging ever since Ellie had started staying over night with Helen occasionally and now the gossip was rampant.

As soon as Helen sent out the invitations to the wedding the gossip stopped. Most of the gossips were invited to the wedding.

The honeymoon was a four-day trip down to Amarillo.

Neither of them considered leaving Ellie at home with a sitter, so the three of them went to Amarillo for three days of shopping, sightseeing, and for Joe and Helen, loving, after Ellie, who was usually exhausted, went to sleep. Ellie always went to sleep early and slept soundly.

So Joe and Helen had their private time together and they left their honeymoon hotel more in love than when they had arrived.

The next week Helen moved some of the things that she wanted to keep into Joe's house and arranged to have an auction for the rest.

The three of them were a family..

Helen's house sold quickly and she was comfortably at home in Joe's house.

Eighteen months later Roy was born.

Ellie was almost eight.

Joe was almost fifty-one.

Helen was thirty-five.

Chapter 3

Linda 1

Linda gathered up her mementos and a few personal belongings from her desk, two or three receipts from recent purchases, a letter from an aunt in Wisconsin, pens, pencils, paper weights, etc'. She put the stuff in a heavy plastic bag.

Lucille, her best friend at the office, peeked around the corner of her cubicle and then stepped in. She could see the tears in Linda's eyes. She said, "Oh, Linda, I wish you wouldn't go. But I understand." And she gave her a little hug. "Bill was hoping you wouldn't go too you know."

Bill was the office manager. Linda had had two lunch dates with him before she met Jeff. From then on it was just Jeff.

Linda said, "Lucille, you have been my very best friend from my first day here, but I can't stay in Litchfield. There are just too many bad memories here. I have to try to get on with my life. I've sold the house and furniture and Jeff's pickup." She dabbed at her eyes with a napkin, sniffed, and said, "I'm keeping my old Escort, and that's about all. It's too painful. I'll have my clothes and a few wedding gifts from the family that I'll keep. That's all. My stuff is already loaded in the car."

Lucille took her hand, the one that was not holding the plastic bag, and said, "Linda we all wish you the best of luck. Please write or call to let us know where you are."

Linda promised she would call and then made her way through the office acknowledging the waves and shaking the hands that were offered from the people at the nearby desks. At the door she turned and felt the tears well up. She then turned again quickly and left.

As she walked across the parking lot, a low rumble of thunder rolled in from the distant west. It was a menacing sound. She looked that direction and saw a long low cloudbank. It had looked that way off and on for two or three days. She remembered the morning weather report saying, "More rain is expected for the entire Midwest."

Well, she was just going to drive west and stay aware of conditions. She wasn't overly concerned about the weather, and her mind was too preoccupied with the recent tragedy in her life for her to become too anxious about something as unpredictable as the weather.

Jeff's death at the hands of terrorists in Spain was so useless, so terrible. He was only going to be there five days. He went as a favor to his boss, whose wife was due to have a baby sometime during that five-day period. He was to just get a computer system up and running in the new office the company was opening. It was going to handle the payroll for the civilian employees. There was no reason to expect any danger.

Jeff was killed along with four other people. One was Jeff's friend Ralph. Both bodies were flown home for interment in the Catholic cemetery just one block from Jeff and Linda's home. Neither casket was opened.

Jeff's company took care of all the expenses and most of the arrangements. Jeff had a quite large insurance policy, which was paid immediately.

Linda was handed Jeff's wedding ring and his high school class ring the day of the funeral. His clothes, his wallet, and other incidentals arrived three days later.

She climbed into the Escort and looked back at the office where she had worked for the last two years. The tears streamed down her face as she pulled out of the parking lot and onto the street. Lucille and Dottie and Theresa were waving from the open door. Lucille was holding her hanky to her nose.

Linda's tears flowed freely. Two blocks later she pulled to the side of the street. She rested her forehead on the steering wheel, wiped her eyes once more and said aloud, "I must get hold of myself." With that she dabbed at her eyes again, blew her nose, and restarted the engine. She purposefully pulled back into the line of traffic and headed west out of town.

Life would go on.

She drove steadily toward the menacing dark clouds stopping once to consult a road map. After studying the map a few minutes she decided to leave the interstate. She was in no particular hurry. It would be nice to drive at a leisurely pace. It would give her time to think. She had no plan, except to head to Colorado where she had once spent two weeks on a happy, carefree vacation, before she met Jeff. Maybe the lighthearted, carefree, atmosphere would help erase the unhappy, bittersweet memories of her recent tragedy.

She would drive the small two lane roads and see the country.

This decision seemed to brighten her outlook somewhat, but again she noticed the threatening clouds in the west. She thought, optimistically, it would probably clear up by morning.

She passed through small towns and villages. She stopped about three thirty in the afternoon for a Coke, and to use the bathroom. It was then that the station manager called her attention to the right front tire. It was a little low on air pressure.

That morning she had dressed in tan slacks, and a light yellow short-sleeved top that was just a little too tight. The station manager wanted to admire the view as long as possible, so he didn't hurry putting air in the tire. His pointed stare made Linda quite uncomfortable.

She thanked the man and hurriedly got in the car and drove away. She promised herself she would dress differently tomorrow.

At five o-clock she decided she would look for a motel in the next town. It was almost six when she rolled into a Drury Inn Motel.

She parked beside a big four-wheel drive pickup. It was like the one Jeff had but a different color. This one was silver.

She checked in, got her room key, and asked about the restaurant across the street. She was assured the food was excellent and reasonably priced. She retrieved one small bag from the car and then locked it. She checked the number on the key and went to her room to shower and put on some different clothes. She would wear something that would be a little less revealing than the yellow shirt. She was used to admiring glances, but the lewd, leering looks that she had gotten from the man at the station repulsed her.

She had only packed a few things in the small bag so the selection was limited. She chose a pair of black knit pants and a dark forest green, long sleeved, silk blouse with four buttons and a small tie at the top. This outfit gave her a dressed up feeling every time she wore it.

With that decision made she ran the tub three fourths full of hot water and stepped in.

Darn it, everything kept reminding her of Jeff. Especially, that silver pickup she'd parked beside when she drove in, even though it was a different color than the dark green of Jeff's. It was probably at least one, and maybe two years older. But it looked well kept and polished like Jeff always kept his.

And now in the bathtub she remembered their honeymoon, and the many romantic times they'd had in motels, hotels, and on weekend camping trips. Those memories kept falling around her like the raindrops that were falling outside the motel window.

"Dammit! She had to stop this!"

"It's over! Finished! I will live on. But it will be different," she told herself, aloud.

She made herself think about the road, the rain, and Colorado. She would need to study the map a little more--and that right front tire?

She finally got her mind and her thoughts under control, got out of the tub and dressed and combed her hair. It was not quite shoulder length with just a little curl and easy to take care of. She applied a little make up and noted it was still raining, so she decided to make a dash to the car and grab an umbrella.

She only got a little wet unlocking the car, and the raindrops sparkled in her hair making it even prettier.

She crossed the street to the restaurant and was escorted to a table by the maitre d, who was obviously impressed with her appearance. The table was near the window looking back across the street at the motel parking lot. After she ordered she sat sipping on the small goblet of white wine and looking out at the rain.

As she watched, a young athletic appearing man ran out to the silver pickup, grabbed something out of the cab and ran back into the motel.

She had only ordered a salad and a tuna sandwich so she was soon finished with her meal. She signaled for the check and left the money plus a tip on the table.

When she got to the door, the same young man that had ran out to the pickup met her at the door. He ducked under the awning out of the rain and stood back quickly and opened the door and held it open for Linda. She murmured a quiet thank you as she walked by and opened her umbrella. As she was opening the umbrella he was thinking, "This is really a classy looking, pretty girl."

Linda stepped out onto the sidewalk thinking, "That guy will be a good catch for someone. He's nice and good looking too."

When she got to her room she started to prepare for bed. She selected the clothes she would wear tomorrow and repacked her bag for an early start.

She was a little distracted by the surprising but not unwelcome sensation she had experienced as she walked past the good looking guy in the doorway of the restaurant.

She watched the weather on T.V. for a few minutes then went to bed.

She slept peacefully and awakened early feeling well rested. It was still raining. She said to herself, "I'll get an early start and maybe I can be through the rain by tomorrow evening."

She dressed in jeans, a white cotton blouse, and one of Jeff's flannel shirts. The shirt was much too large for her but she felt comfortable wearing it. Jeff never really liked the shirt. Actually it was too large for him and he didn't like the color very well. It was red and white plaid with small yellow and blue lines running through it. Jeff thought it was too light. Linda really liked the color. She seldom buttoned it but wore it open and rolled the sleeves up to her elbows. Somehow, her dark blonde hair and her light brown eyes became even more attractive when she wore that color.

Chapter 4

Linda 2

She had watched the weather channel last night and knew that it was a large area that had been getting heavy rain for several days. The commentator talked at length about the serious flooding and about the dikes and levees that were threatened by the force of the water that kept rising against them. The station had a lot of footage of the increasing amount of debris that was being carried down the rivers. Trees, parts of buildings, and even a few animals that had been trapped in low places were to be seen floating down with the angry waters

Several roads were closed because of the flooding so Linda consulted her map to see if her intended route was all right. It appeared to be O.K. She knew some of the smaller roads that appeared as just thin blue lines on the map would be closed, but her chosen route seemed to be clear.

She packed the small suitcase and went to the desk and signed the credit card slip. She briefly discussed the weather with the two ladies at the desk and then carried the bag out to the car.

The rain had let up a little. She noticed the silver pickup was still parked in he same spot. She kind of wished she could meet someone like the guy she had met in the doorway of the restaurant last night. She thought, "He must surely be the driver of that silver pickup." The thought quickened her heartbeat. She felt a pleasant surprise. It was O.K.

She backed out of the parking space and turned toward the highway.

She had decided to stop at a fast food place for a coffee and an Egg McMuffin and eat as she drove. She wanted to get out of the rain and flooding as soon as possible.

As soon as she got on the street she felt a tug in the steering, a slight pull to the right. It had to be that right front tire. She spotted a self-serve gas station just ahead and pulled up to the air hose. Luckily, it was under the canopy and out of the rain that was still falling steadily.

She'd had a little experience with this sort of thing when she was in high school and college. Using the built in gage, she quickly brought he pressure up to thirty-five pounds and replaced the valve cap and drove on down to Mc Donald's drive up window. She got the coffee and Egg McMuffin and was soon on her way.

Shortly after nine A.M. the rain had stopped. The sky was still overcast and farther to the west it still looked threatening but for the moment there was no rain. Occasionally the sun peeped through for a minute or two.

Linda relaxed a little and enjoyed the rolling countryside

The radio was playing a combination of early 1960's rock and modern country and frequently reporting on the weather conditions in Illinois, Iowa and Missouri. There was serious flooding in all three states.

Linda turned off the radio and ran through a patch of sunlight, but the western sky still looked dark and ominous. She checked the gas gage as she thought to herself, "I'd better gas up. If I remember the map right, it's a long stretch to the next town."

She had just passed a "Gas 'n Eat" sign, so she said aloud, "I'll stop there."

As she rounded the next curve, she saw the place. It was a decent looking place; two rows of two gas pump islands, a restaurant and a quick stop grocery store in a newly painted concrete block building.

Linda thought, "I hope they have a nice restroom. I expect it will be more than an hour before I see another one."

The road had been a little rough the last few miles, so she had not noticed the slight pull of the steering wheel until she drove onto the new concrete driveway. She coasted up to the nearest pump and busied herself rearranging some of the things in the back seat before she started into the store. It was then she noticed the silver pickup as it drove in and pulled up to the other pump island. It was the same one she had parked beside last night and the same young man that had opened the door for her at the restaurant.

She was suddenly glad to see him. She didn't know why but there was this exciting, stirring sensation in her chest or stomach that she welcomed, an old familiar feeling of desire that had eluded her since Jeff's death.

Then her mind jerked her back to the right front tire.

Chapter 5

Saturday Morning

Roy had chosen the small two lane side roads rather than the interstates because he just wasn't in the mood to maintain the pace it would take to stay with the flow of early summer vacation traffic. A glance at the fuel gage made him decide to make a stop at the next gas station.

As he cruised along he only half noticed the slightly rolling countryside. He was deep in his thoughts of his so recently disrupted life. He had been comfortable and very happy in their new home.

Mary Ann, and their little girl, ten-month-old Dorothy Ann, had been the perfect young family.

But he had to stop thinking about that. It was over. The freak icy patch on the road in late March had, it seemed, ended his life as well. He had begun to realize that life would go on. He knew he would have to sell the house that he and Mary Ann had been so proud of.

Roy got through the next month in a daze. But by mid May he had only tried to sleep there in their house three nights since that terrible day.

Mrs. Olson's boarding house had been a place to crash when he became so exhausted that work was nearly impossible.

A fleeting road sign caught his attention just in time to read, Gas 3 mi. Thankfully, the sign jarred him out of his emotionally destructive memories.

He rounded a curve and saw another sign, Gas 'n Eat At Ed's.

Roy wasn't really hungry but he did need fuel and maybe a little snack for the road would be O.K.

The rain had stopped for the moment but the sky was still looking dark and foreboding in the west.

It was only a little after ten A.M., but there weren't many towns of any size for several miles so a stop here would be a good idea.

The road straightened out after the next curve and there was a big new sign announcing, Ed's Place.

As he rolled up to the pumps Roy noticed a two or three year old blue Ford Escort. What got his attention was how heavily it was loaded. It sat heavy on the springs and a large cardboard box in the passenger seat almost obscured the driver. The back seat was also piled high with neatly stacked boxes and clothing.

"Somebody moving," he thought, as he busied himself with the gas cap and the pump nozzle. He got the gasoline flowing and was cleaning the windshield when the driver of the Escort came around the front of her car. She looked vaguely familiar?

She was tall, maybe 5' 9", slender, honey blonde hair, and darned good looking. She looked worried or maybe serious was a better word but definitely concerned about something.

As she walked by on her way into the store, she looked at Roy's pickup and then directly at Roy. When their eyes met there was a flicker of recognition.

Roy watched her walk past as he finished cleaning the mirror on the driver's side of the pickup. He watched over the hood as she took the last few steps and disappeared into the store. "This is the same girl I saw last night!" he said, aloud to himself. He sure liked the way she moved.

Suddenly, Roy was shocked to realize how this girl, with her worried look and her pretty light brown eyes, had affected him. He had hardly noticed any other woman since the accident.

Well, she was certainly worth a second look from anybody.

He finished filling his tank and checked the oil. As he was putting the hood down, she came back out of the store closely followed by a young attendant. He was saying, "I'll check the oil and the tires too." There was no doubt the young man had noticed her attractiveness, as Roy had, and he was anxious to impress her.

She was saying to the boy, "I think I may have a low tire on the right front. I've had to have air put in it twice since yesterday noon. I hope it's not leaking slowly from a small puncture." The boy said, "I hope not too, Ma'am, 'cause we don't have any way to fix 'em here, but I'll put air in it." He wiped his greasy hands on a greasier shop rag and reached for the air hose.

The girl put her hand to her forehead with a worried look, and asked, How far to the next place where I could get it repaired?"

"If you're going west through the bottoms it would be about 25 miles, if you're going east it's about 17 miles back to the last big town you passed through. That's the only two places I know about," he replied.

Roy had watched this exchange with more than a casual interest. He couldn't stop thinking how pretty she was even with that worried frown on her face. He stepped around the front of his pickup and a thought entered his mind. "Maybe it's not a puncture? It could just be a valve leak." He walked ahead, around to the front of the Escort and squatted down to look at the questionable tire. It looked like an almost new tire. He stood up and noticed the girl watching him closely.

The attendant was just starting to put air in the tire. He gauged the pressure and then he added a little more air and checked it again.

Roy stepped closer to the young lady, and asked, "Ma'am, would you mind if I checked that valve stem? That could be the problem."

She looked at the attendant, and then looked back at Roy with a somewhat startled expression, "Why, I guess not," she said, and looked at the boy again for support.

He stammered, "Well. Yeah. I guess that won't hurt nothin."

Roy squatted down again and unscrewed the valve cap that the boy had just reinstalled. He then spit a little saliva on his forefinger and applied it to the valve stem. Immediately bubbles started to form on his finger and on the valve stem, clearly indicating a substantial leak.

"That's the trouble, Ma'am," Roy said. "I think it's just loose and I think I can fix it. I'll get a valve tool to tighten the stem and that should stop the leak."

He went back to his pickup, to the large toolbox in the open bed of the truck. He unlocked the padlock that secured the lid. When he opened the box, it revealed a neat assortment of tools of all description. He removed the top tray and dug down among the screwdrivers, pliers, chisels, punches, and other miscellaneous tools in the bottom of the box and found the valve tool.

He started back to the Escort. Linda was standing there expectantly.

He noticed again the attractive, feminine way she stood there, uncertain what to do about this polite, good natured, good looking stranger and his confident offer of help. As he crossed the driveway to her car, he took note of her oversized shirt, obviously a man's shirt, a light red and white plaid with the sleeves rolled to just below the elbows and worn unbuttoned on the outside of lightly faded blue jeans.

Roy thought, "That big shirt is not doing a very good job of hiding a very good figure. This girl sure is pretty, even dressed like that."

Linda was thinking, "He certainly seems sure of himself and he seems very nice."

Roy again squatted down beside the offending tire. Roy quickly inserted the valve tool into the valve stem and gave it a firm clockwise twist. He removed the tool and again applied saliva to the valve stem.

No Bubbles!

He replaced the cap on the stem and stood up, saying, "Ma'am, I believe that fixed the problem. You shouldn't have any more trouble."

The young attendant said, "That's right, Ma'am. That'll take care of that, I'll bet, and your oil is O.K. and I'll clean your windshield too." He was trying to regain some credibility with her, and Linda felt obligated to acknowledge his efforts. "Thank you very much," she said, "and the windshield certainly does need cleaning."

As Roy turned toward his truck, Linda stepped forward and touched his arm. "Oh, Sir, er ah, Mister, I, ah."

"The name's Roy, Ma'am," he said with a grin.

"Well, I would like to pay you for your help. I'm so glad to get it fixed."

"Oh, no, Ma'am. Don't even consider it. I couldn't accept payment for that. It was nothing."

"But I was afraid I wouldn't be able to make it to a repair shop even if I turned back."

Roy grinned and said, "Now you won't have to worry. Just consider it an anonymous favor. I enjoy doing favors for folks. I've been the receiver of a few my self. So, no charge."

Linda smiled at Roy thinking, "He really has a nice grin and he seems so sincere." Then she caught herself. "I haven't felt like this in months, but he really is a likeable guy. Maybe my life could be good again."

She said, "Well, thanks a lot. I surely do appreciate it very much."

She became aware of a lighthearted feeling and a warm sensation spreading all through her body, even as a cold rain began to fall.

As Roy turned again toward the store and his truck, she watched the easy way he walked. She thought he looked very nice, with his broad shoulders and his straight back. His dark hair was short, beneath a brown baseball cap with a construction company logo on the front. She didn't know a thing about him but she couldn't help but like him.

Then she thought, regretfully, "I'll probably never see him again." She remembered the firm feel of his arm when she had touched him. There was still a warm feeling in her fingertips.

Linda went ahead to her car and topped off her gas tank. The boy was just finishing the windshield and had it sparkling. He said, "I'm sure glad that guy came along 'cause we don't even have a valve tool."

Linda said, "It certainly was nice of him to fix it, and I thank you very much for your efforts too."

She paid him for the gas, looking for Roy to come back out of the store. Yes, that's right, Roy. He'd said his name was Roy. She wouldn't forget that! She lingered a while straightening the things in the back seat just to kill a little time hoping Roy would come out.

She realized she wanted to see him again just to confirm the feelings she was experiencing. There was definitely an attraction but he still had not come out.

It was raining a little harder now. Linda slowly got into her car still watching the store. She really didn't want to leave without seeing him again. She was very grateful to him for fixing the tire, but there was something more. The slow, easy way he talked and moved gave her a comfortable secure feeling.

She slowly pulled back on to the highway. There was hardly any traffic on the road. This suited Linda just fine. She didn't like driving in a lot of traffic and this would give her time and space to sort out these unexpected feelings. These sensations were not unwelcome, but she was surprised at their intensity.

Roy entered the store. He wandered around among the displays of junk foods and finally selected two packages of snack crackers, one peanut butter, and one cheese. He liked to alternate the two flavors. He already had at least six, or maybe seven, 20 oz. plastic bottles of Pepsi in the large 120- quart cooler in the back of the pickup. The cooler was a holdover from the days of block parties and picnics. It would have been gone with the rest of their belongings at the auction but it had been forgotten in the bed of the pickup.

He also remembered, Mrs. Olson had said she was putting something in the cooler while he was stowing stuff behind the seat and in the cab. Whatever? There was plenty of space in that large sturdy cooler.

He took the snack crackers to the counter and laid them by the cash register. The woman behind the counter rang them up and asked,

"Are you going west?"

Roy counted out the money and answered, "Yep, to west Kansas, to see my folks."

"Have you heard about the flooding?" She asked. "It's all across Illinois and pretty bad they say." She went on with her unsolicited weather report. "They've had three or four more inches of rain up river last night and it's supposed to start here again by 11:00 o-clock and we're already soaked." She paused for a breath and Roy said,

"I heard the weather report this morning and they thought the flood crest would reach the interstate in about 36 hours. By nightfall I should be in Missouri."

"Well, it's flooding there too, my uncle called last night. He lives just nine miles into Missouri; he says it's terrible, water everywhere!" she said excitedly!

Roy turned toward the door, and she said, "Be careful, and good luck," as he walked out.

Chapter 6

Sam Burkett's office

Sam Burkett had his crew assembled that Saturday morning and the situation was serious. Sam had been road boss for eleven years and this was the worst time he had faced in all those years. Lives were in danger. He didn't want to send any of his men out today but he had to have first hand information. Some roads were already closed. Parts of some of the roads were still open but the water was still rising swiftly, and when the water covered these roads, they would have to be barricaded as soon as the road crew could get there.

Sam spoke to the group. "Boys, we've got us a pretty tough situation here. We've got to keep as many roads open as we can, but if there is water going over a road, even very shallow water, we've got to close it."

"Now, Richard, you and Jimmie take # 30, and load her with barricade material and git out to roads 9, 10, and 11. There's not any water over # 11 yet but there's gonna' be. And if that big levee over at Bridgton gives away, I wouldn't want to be anywhere near that three mile stretch of road on this side of the bridge. Keep in touch on the two way radio. Close all three of 'em."

Sam continued, "Now Charlie and Bill have been running the back roads on patrol since midnight, so I'm going to send them home to rest up, 'cause most of us may be bagging sand tonight."

"Andy, you an' Mose go home too. Figure on doin' road patrol tonight. We've got to know what's going on out there twenty-four hours a day."

Sam went ahead and dispatched two more crews to other parts of the county to close roads and report on conditions.

He said, "I'm gonna' keep Wilford and Dusty here to cover any emergencies. Be careful boys. These gravel roads are awful soft. I've already got two complaints from folks who have been hung up right in the middle of the road. So call in and tell me what's happening."

Sam told Dusty and Wilford to check out the remaining three vehicles, one more pickup and two large dump trucks. They needed them to be ready to go at a moment's notice.

Sam stayed busy in the office taking care of the annoying paper work that he didn't like, but still had to be done.

The radio stayed quiet until almost 10:30. It crackled to life with the usual squawk.

And then Richard's voice, "Sam, send one of the dump trucks with a heavy chain--

Sam cut in.

"What happened, Rich?"

Richard's voice again, "You know that culvert we fixed in April, 'bout a half mile south of road 10? It caved in! There's been so much water run off from that big field up hill it washed out under the culvert and when our back wheels hit it, it just caved in. The rear of the truck bed is almost sitting on the black top."

Sam cut in again, " Rich, can you get a chain on it?"

Richard said, "Yeah, we can tie on to the trailer hitch. Throw in a couple 'a planks, so we can roll the front wheels over the cave in. We'll need two more barricades too. This road is definitely closed and we haven't even got to # 11 yet."

Sam said, "Will and Dusty are on the way but get to # 11 as soon as you can. The weather people at Bridgton say that big levee upstream from the bridge has reached the critical stage."

Richard gave Sam a 10-4 and clicked off to wait for Wilford and Dusty.

Sam's phone rang. Sam always answered the same way. "County Road office, Sam speaking."

The caller said, "Sam, this is Fred over at Bridgton. This river situation is getting scary. I don't think the dike is going to hold 'till dark. It can't possibly hold another 10 inches, and that's what the forecasters are saying we're going to get by morning."

Fred Robbins and Sam had been friends for years even though in different states. Their offices were only about 25 miles apart and Fred was the road commissioner for his county, as Sam was in his. They often compared notes and swapped stories.

Fred said, "Sam, your situation is worse than mine and I just want to offer my help if there is anything I can do. Whatever you do, be careful. This river is treacherous."

"I believe you," Sam replied, "and I sure do appreciate the offer but I can't see any way, anyone can hold back this old river when she gets on a rampage like this. I'm sure there is big trouble on the way."

Fred said, "You're right, of course, but I just wanted you to know I'm concerned and wanted to offer my help, and to wish you good luck."

Sam said, "Well, thanks a lot, Fred. We'll all just do the best we can and you be careful too." And they hung up.

As soon as they hung up, Sam punched the transmit button on the two-way radio. "Base calling truck # 30, come in 30. Do you read me, Richard?"

Richard's voice came on immediately. "Yeah, Sam, we're still waiting for a pull."

Sam said, "Richard, work as fast as you can, git that truck out of there, put up a barricade there, then high tail it back to the first road cast, then to the first road south, to Road Eleven. Git that road closed! I think big trouble is coming. Tell the boys in the dump truck to follow you in case there would be another problem."

"O. K., Sam," Richard replied, "We don't think it will take long to get it out. We'll just drag the rear wheels up on solid black top, and then lay the planks down to roll the front wheels across and we'll be out. We've been checking and we don't think there is any damage at all. So we'll be rolling in thirty minutes or less after they get here."

"O.K., boys, that sounds good. Don't get caught in any low spots. If, or when, that old levee goes, there will be Hell to pay."

Across the river in Bridgton folks were becoming increasingly vigilant and aware of the seriousness of the situation. Almost everyone in town had friends or relatives across the river. If that big levee failed, there would be widespread devastation.

The levee, built some 50 years before, had never been threatened. It was immense, a huge earthen dike built by the Army Corp of Engineers. It was thirty feet high for almost 4 miles and proclaimed by the engineers to be impregnable. The levee had always been well maintained but no one expected it to ever be tested to this degree. The large amount of debris floating down the river was beginning to build up on the under structure of the bridge, thereby putting more pressure against the earthen dike.

Chapter 7

Later Saturday Morning

Roy went out to his pickup thinking about the girl. He was glad he had been able to help her. Just seeing her had brightened his day. "But," he said, "I'll probably never see her again." That thought disturbed him as he got into the pickup. He started the engine, thinking, "I don't even know which direction she went, but if I did, I'd be tempted to follow her just for the chance to see her and maybe talk to her again."

He suddenly felt like a schoolboy about to ask a girl for a date for the first time. "This is silly," he thought, "I'm an ex husband, and a father." That thought brought him back to reality sharply. It was the first time he had forgotten his wife and little daughter for even a little while. They were always there in the back of his mind, but he was letting them go a little at a time. He knew he must get on with his life.

Roy put the truck in gear and eased back onto the highway. He turned on the radio to distract himself from thinking about the past. It was a country music station playing a tune he knew from four or five years ago when he had played rhythm guitar in a small country band. He had not yet, at that time met Mary Ann, so it was safe to think about that and he hummed along having forgotten most of the lyrics.

The road curved around through hills and woods. This area was not heavily populated but a few nice farmhouses dotted the hills here and there. It was still raining steadily, not hard, but it kept the windshield wipers slapping rapidly. Once when he topped a large hill a long valley appeared on the left, and at the far end of the valley it widened out to expose a great expanse of water. Roy said to himself, "That must be some of the flooding the weather people are talking about."

It was near 11:00 o-clock on Saturday morning and the music on the radio stopped. A male voice broke in saying, "This is Randy Harris, from the news room at station KMTR, St. Louis. The station has sent me up here to Bridgton, to monitor and report on this flooding situation. It's very serious folks. This is the first time in the recorded history of this town that the river stage has reached this level. It is far above any previous reading. It is definitely the first time that this huge dike has been threatened. The Army Corp of Engineers declared it to be the tallest, longest, strongest earthen dike in the entire Midwest, and equal to the task it was designed to do. But, people, it is in jeopardy! Some local engineers think it won't hold 'til morning."

"Now, I'm going to sign off for a while. I've contracted for a cherry picker to be driven over here from your Miller Construction Company. It's going to elevate me forty feet into the air right here at the edge of the water. I will actually be suspended over the edge of the water just a little but I will be forty feet up. From there I will be able to see for miles and I will try to describe in detail this drama that is unfolding."

"I will be back on the air in approximately 25 minutes. Thank you."

With that announcement the music came back on and Roy flipped the radio off. "This must be big news," he mused, "and it must be getting bigger."

He drove on 4 or 5 more miles, thinking, "I must be getting close to the river. I'll be glad to get on the other side."

He had just passed a cross road and he noted it was South Cemetery Road and he was on West Road Eleven. In about a half mile he topped a hill and there it was. Miles of water! The road was straight for more than three miles. The roadbed was built up about 4 feet above the surrounding terrain and straight as a string for all of those three miles. There was water on both sides of the road, but about 2 feet below the surface of the road.

Across that three miles through the haze, Roy saw what he thought must be that huge levee they were talking about and the super structure of the bridge.

Then he noticed what was probably a car, a little more than half way across. "I think it is a blue car? And I don't think it is moving," he said aloud.

There was so much to see of that immense lake and the far shoreline and the great levee that he hadn't immediately seen the car. Now he was closer; he could see the hood was up. Someone wearing a raincoat was standing beside it.

It was the girl! And the blue Escort! With the leaky tire!

Chapter 8

Linda Is Trapped

About twenty minutes earlier Linda had topped that same hill. She gasped and drew a sharp breath when that panorama unfolded before her.

"This is scary!" she said aloud, to herself. "But there were no warning signs so it must be O.K. That's an awful lot of water, but I can see the road all the way across so it must be all right."

She thought, "I can be through this stretch in less than five minutes."

Having rationalized her fears away and seeing the long straight road ahead and seeing no on coming traffic, she pressed her foot down on the accelerator and increased her speed from the 45 or 50 miles per hour she had been driving to near 60. That's when she noticed odor of hot radiator fluid. She became alarmed and very sensitive to the way the engine sounded. It was a different sound, or vibration. She soon knew. Something was definitely wrong. Again she spoke aloud to herself, "If I can just get across this long straight stretch, I'll pull in to the first place that has a phone and call a tow truck."

That thought had hardly left her mind when the vibration increased greatly and she found she could not maintain her speed. In fact, it had dropped to less than 30 miles per hour and was dropping steadily. And then the engine stopped completely!

She coasted to a stop in her lane. There was no shoulder to drive onto. The water was virtually the edge of the road.

She did not panic or become upset. She just wished if this had to happen she would have preferred it had happened somewhere else.

She smiled at the ridiculous wish. "Obviously, it would have been more convenient if it had happened in front of a repair shop. An automobile repair shop, to be specific."

She smiled again and then became serious. "Someone will come along soon and I'll hitch a ride to the town just across the river. I think it's called Bridgton. And then I'll send a tow truck to haul it in."

Linda looked around. She had stopped right beside some trees. She looked ahead and she looked behind. Those three trees were the only objects, beside the road, that stuck up out of the water.

"This is still scary," she said aloud to herself again. "This has got me talking to myself, but someone will come along soon," she repeated to reassure herself. She raised the hood knowing there was nothing she could do to correct the problem, but it would alert anyone driving by from either direction that there was a problem.

It was still raining lightly so she put on a light raincoat over the large shirt she was wearing, over the short-sleeved white blouse. The raincoat had a hood attached so she flipped it up to protect her hair. She walked around the car, to better look in all directions. There was barely room to walk on the side next to the water. She had pulled as far to the right as she dared, and that left little space between the car and the water.

On the third trip around she saw a vehicle pop over the hill about a mile and a half behind. "Good," she said. "I hope whoever it is, is a friendly person. They surely wouldn't leave me stranded out here."

She stepped to the side of the car next to the center of the road preparing to flag the oncoming car.   But it wasn't a car. It was a pickup truck. *A Silver Pickup Truck!* Could it be the same one, the one with the super nice driver? Oh! She hoped so! He was so nice, and so good looking, and so virile. She caught herself, "What was she thinking?" She blushed.

By this time the truck was rolling to a stop behind her car.

Chapter 9

Enter Randy Harris

Over in Bridgton, Randy Harris was about ready to start broadcasting again. Troy Williams, the cherry picker operator from the construction company, was telling him,

"We'll have to delay this caper until the wind dies down, or not go very high. With this much wind it would be dangerous to go even twenty feet."

Troy was in his mid forties, about 5' 10" and 170 pounds, strong built and with an all business demeanor. Dressed in the tan work uniform, the short-sleeved shirt with the Miller Construction Co. Logo and his name over the left breast pocket, and a baseball cap with the logo, and the sturdy work shoes, he gave the impression that he could handle the job.

Randy said, "I just talked to Jack, the weather man at the station, and he says the wind won't quit here, but it should let up considerably sometime in the next 45 minutes. Maybe the rain will decrease too. I hope."

Troy said, "We can go up in the rain but a big gust of wind from the right angle could blow us over if we were up 35 or 40 ft."

Randy drummed his fingers on the small desktop. They were sitting in the KMTR station van and Randy was anxious to resume his broadcast as soon as possible. A conversation he had a few minutes ago with a city engineer caused him think the levee may not hold much longer. There was no more conversation for a few minutes as they both listened to the wind and the rain beating on the roof of the van. Suddenly they both looked up. There was a change and the rain had almost stopped. Randy jerked the van door open.

"Jack was almost right," he said, "there is some open sky up there, just a few drops falling now. I think it is going to stop completely."

"Yeah, and look. The wind has died down to almost nothing so we can go up now," Troy said.

Randy replied, "That's great, but Jack did say the rain and wind both would be intermittent so we'll have to beware of sudden gusts. Now I'll get back on the air as soon as I can, and we will "levitate!"

With that he jumped back into the van and started pushing buttons and throwing switches.

In less than two minutes he was ready to start broadcasting. He would use the remote mike with the little tail antennae. The engineer back at KMTR was standing by with the old Country / Bluegrass song "Raining In Missouri" going out over the air.

At Randy's signal he would flip the switch that would send Randy's voice out over KMTR as well as the local radio station in Bridgton.

Randy hopped out of the van and strode briskly to where Troy was waiting. He said, "O.K., Troy, tell me what to do and where to stand."

"Well, Randy, just climb into the bucket. There is not much room in here for two people, but there is enough. Don't worry if it wobbles around some. Just hang on and I'll take'er up slow."

Randy said, "O.K., I'm going on the air now."

Randy inserted his earpiece and gave the signal that he was ready to go, and instantly he heard through the earpiece,

"Go, Randy."

He started to speak. "O.K., folks, this is Randy Harris on the air again, coming to you through Station KMTR, St Louis, and the local station right here in Bridgton. Nearly 30 minutes ago I told you I would be going up in a cherry picker to get a bird's eye view of this spectacular flood. At this moment I am entering the bucket of this machine preparing to ascend. Oh! Excuse me, Troy. Folks, this really is not much more than a bucket, and it's pretty close quarters for two. Sorry, Troy, but now I think we are situated. Troy Williams will handle the controls."

"First of all we are located at the east end of Water Street. The street dead ends right here at the water's edge. When this huge new levee was constructed around 1950, this street was the entrance to the bridge, which at that time spanned this mighty river carrying traffic to and from the great farming community across the river. The road that led from the old bridge to cross that fertile valley on the east side of the river has long since been closed. There are only two or three dilapidated old buildings remaining that would hint at where the old road had been."

"A new bridge was built at the behest of the Army Corp of Engineers in 1953. And the new road on the other side of the river was built up to a height of four feet above the valley floor so traffic could still move freely, even in times of heavy rain. But this prolonged streak of extremely wet weather is severely testing the system."

"The new bridge is located about a mile south of Water Street where we are now. There is quite a lot of traffic here at this time, slow automobile traffic. Sightseers and pedestrians line the fence along the promenade for a block on each side of Water Street. There is a tension in the air. There is an air of expectancy. I feel it. Something terrible is about to happen. The people are nervously milling about. They know they are helpless, powerless. There is nothing they can do to stop this invincible force that grows more dangerous and destructive by the hour."

"Do you have that feeling, Troy?" Randy asked, holding the microphone over to Troy.

"Yes, I do," Troy replied. "I don't really feel that the town of Bridgton is in any danger, but there is much concern for people on the other side of that big levee."

"That's right, Troy, and the folks that live in the low ground on the south and west of Bridgton are in a dangerous position, and the water just keeps rising. Some people have already been evacuated. If the predictions hold true, the water levels could rise another ten inches in the next 24 hours."

"Well, it's time to have a look at this phenomenal flood. We will go up 35 or 40 feet unless the wind kicks up again."

"OOPS! Here we go. Troy says we will go up slowly, and I will try to describe the scene as we go. Even at ten feet up this is spectacular. I can see far up and down the river and we can hear the rushing water from up here, even better than we could while still on the ground. It's almost a dull roar. There is also a distinct odor that I did not notice while I was on the ground, a strange fishy odor mingled with uprooted vegetation, and--and, uh— putrefaction. Yeah, that's it. It must be the several dead animals we have seen and heard about. They have been trapped on islands in the river that have become inundated after the swiftly rising water surrounded them. Many did not escape in the raging currents."

"Troy has stopped our accent here at about 20 feet. Is that about right, Troy? He's nodding yes. At this elevation I am seeing a lot of water across the river covering the low-lying farmland. The fog and mist that is obstructing vision at two or three miles prevents me from seeing anything clearly at two miles or more. The water I'm seeing is not river water; it is runoff water from the hills on the far side of the bottomland. They are hills that I cannot see now because of the haze and fog, but I know they are there."

"Let's go on up, Troy. Those clouds I see moving in might cause the wind to start blowing again and I want to get a better look at that levee before we are forced down."

They started slowly moving up.

"Good God, Troy, look at that! People, this is frightening! It is not the height. I have flown light planes at all elevations for many hours, but this is a terrifying sight! The water is literally at the top of the levee. It cannot possibly hold! There are miles and miles of water. When I look around, the town of Bridgton is an island! If the levee does fail, the water that would rush through the breach would not be diminished for hours. Considering the volume of water that is coming down river, relentlessly, it could be days."

"Ladies and Gentlemen, I apologize. This scene almost leaves me speechless. I know I cannot with mere words cause you to feel the impact of this catastrophe, which is sure to happen. It almost makes me want to look away, but I can't! I am compelled to witness this.

----------*Troy, Look!!! Oh My God!! Get Us Down!! Oh, No! No, Wait!! I must tell what I'm seeing!* "Ladies and Gentlemen, Troy and I just witnessed a most astonishing and terrifying sight. The water was lapping at the very top of the levee as far as we could see up stream, when suddenly the top eight, or maybe as much as ten feet of the levee just slid off and down the far side and was disintegrated by the furious current."

"The length of this initial breach was approximately two hundred feet, but it is much longer now, maybe as much as a thousand feet. The water is roaring through the opening with a terrifying sound. The water level in the river was about twenty-five feet above the runoff water in the field below, and that huge break sent a literal wall of water nearly eight feet high, surging madly across the low land with no restriction. I can still see that wall of water quickly approaching the one road that is still open. That road will very soon be under five or six feet of madly rushing river water. That road is the same road that leads to the new bridge a mile down stream from our vantage point here on Water Street."

"Folks, to witness this, it literally takes your breath away; the heat is oppressive and the scene is so frightening. Troy and I are both soaked with perspiration."

"The water is still roaring through the ever widening breach. It must be five or six hundred yards wide by now, but the water level on the river has not dropped more than a foot down stream from the break. The overwhelming volume of water is surging undiminished down the river channel. The valley across the river will eventually be full and then the current through the valley will slow and the river channel will again carry the main flow."

"Troy, the wind is picking up again and those clouds are looking more threatening all the time."

"Yeah, Randy. We'll have to get down. It looks like it's coming."

Randy continued, " Ladies and gentlemen, I have never felt more inadequate as a news announcer. This has been a very humbling experience. As we descend, I feel almost in shock. What we witnessed was a great force, unleashing itself in the total destruction of that portion of this great levee. It was violent! I am at loss for words."

"The wall of water, as it rushed into that valley, would have crushed any modern dwelling within two or three hundred yards in an instant. It would have reduced it to splinters, to be carried away by the deluge."

"We are down to the ground now and just in time. The wind is getting pretty strong again and here's the rain."

"I'll sign off now knowing that I did not do justice to the stupendous, terrible scene that Troy and I just witnessed."

"This has been Randy Harris from station KMTR St. Louis, Missouri."

Chapter 10

Sam Knows There Will Be Trouble

Sam Burkett was walking the floor muttering to himself. One of the crews had returned to the office, having finished their patrol and were awaiting further orders.

Sam was saying in a grumbling tone, " That damned old river is really going to cause some big problems this time."

Sam had the radio tuned to the Bridgton station and was listening to Randy Harris's live broadcast from the bucket of the cherry picker. Sam knew from Randy's description of the scene that big trouble was inevitable.

Again he mumbled as he paced, "I sure wish Richard would call in and tell me that road 11 west was closed. It would be a killer if anyone was caught out there when that levee gives away."

As if by mental telepathy the radio squawked, and Richard's voice came on.

"Sam, we've got'em all closed and barricaded. We got 11 west about twenty five minutes ago and we've just finished setting up the boards and signs on 10."

"That sounds real good, Richard. Anyone that entered that road twenty-five minutes ago would be safely across by now. Good job, men. You guys come on in now; it'll soon be time for lunch. After lunch we'll check the reports and go from there."

When he returned the mike to the cradle, he heard Randy Harris's terrified exclamation! *"Oh my god! Get us down! Oh, no! No! Wait! I must tell what I am seeing!"*

Sam said, "Oh Shit!" He and the men knew what had happened and could only guess at the consequences.

It was going to be tough.

Sam muttered again, " God help anyone caught in the path of that monster."

Chapter 11

Roy and Linda Meet

Roy's heart jumped as he rolled to a stop behind her car. He grabbed his big over sized Poncho and slipped it on as he ran up to her. "What's the trouble, Ma'am?" he asked.

"Oh, Roy, I don't know! The engine got real hot and wouldn't run any more."

The rain drummed down loudly on the hood of Roy's poncho, but what he heard was this pretty girl with the pretty worried frown on her face using his first name as if she had practiced it.

The boyish thrill he felt was uncharacteristic of him but he didn't care. He realized how very much he had wanted to see her again.

She was clearly as glad to see him, as he was to see her. She was worried about her car and her predicament, but there was something more.

She was standing very close as Roy leaned over to look under the hood. He saw instantly that the fan belt was broken.

There were several options. They could drive to the next town and send a tow truck back to tow it in. He could drive into the next town, buy a belt and come back and install it, which would be no problem for Roy with his knowledge of mechanics. Or they could try to push or tow it in, which would be pretty tricky even with two experienced drivers, and Linda said she'd never tried to do anything like that.

Roy had an almost irresistible desire to just take her in his arms and hold her, but instead he explained the options.

She appeared to be mulling over the possibilities when Roy hesitantly said, "Ma'am, you know my name, but I don't know yours. And I sure would like to know your name, your address, your phone number, and everything."

After he got started just everything came out at once, things he had wanted to know ever since he had held the door of the restaurant open for her, really since the first time he saw her.

Linda drew a sharp breath and smiled, "Why, Roy, it's Linda. Linda Powers, but just now I don't have an address or a phone number. I'm moving. I just don't know where yet. And I don't know your last name. All you told me was Roy."

Roy grinned and stuck out his hand. "Roy Johnson, Ma'am, er' ah, Linda, Linda Powers. I'm really glad to meet you."

Linda gave him her hand, and Roy held it, a little too long, but she never pulled away. There was electricity in that handshake. Their eyes met and held. In that instant, there was a kind of mutual understanding, a kind of unspoken promise that passed between them.

Their hands and eyes released, slowly, reluctantly.

The radio in Roy's truck was still on, and in that short silence, they could hear Randy Harris's excited voice saying, "The water is literally at the top of the levee! It can't possibly hold!"

They both heard the stirring, excited statement, and Linda said, "This sounds pretty serious."

Roy replied, "We're apparently in a dangerous position here. That levee they are talking about is that levee, there! He pointed straight ahead down the road. It's only a little over a mile ahead. If it gives away, there will be a terrific rush of water across this valley."

"We had better hurry and get your car out of here."

The rain had stopped so Roy took off his poncho, folded it up and stuffed it in the big cooler. Linda was taking off her raincoat at the same time and stowing it in the back seat of her car.

Linda said something that Roy couldn't hear because of the radio, so he reached in and flipped it off. He turned back to hear what Linda had said. She repeated, "I think we should go in to the next town and send a tow truck back for my car."

Roy agreed. "I believe that is the best option. I'll move some things around here in the cab of the pickup to make room for a passenger. If you have some things you want to take along in case the tow truck does not come right away, I'll make room for them."

Linda said, "Do you think I should stay here with my car?" She was hoping Roy would say she should not stay. She liked the idea of getting into that crowded cab with him.

Somehow, she completely trusted Roy and she just liked the idea of being close to him.

Roy answered her question with an emphatic, "Absolutely Not! I wouldn't think of leaving you out here alone. Bring whatever you may want or need, and we will run on in to the next town that has a tow truck."

Linda was thrilled at the protective attitude Roy was taking and she was confident that his concern was genuine.

In her mind Linda knew that this was pretty presumptuous thinking, but she told herself, sometimes, intuition could be stronger than reason.

Roy said, "I'll turn on the four way flasher in your car and we'll leave the hood up as a signal that there is a problem. Do you have your keys?"

Linda said, "I'll get the keys, they're in the ignition."

She grabbed the keys and the small overnight bag she always carried. It contained a bra, one pair of panties, one pair of light pink socks, a light, short sleeved pink sweater, and a pair of beige cotton pants, along with a small assortment of make up, a comb, a brush, a toothbrush and tooth paste, and a plastic bag to hold her soiled clothes.

Linda called it her "Emergency Kit."

She closed and locked the door and slipped the keys into her purse. She walked back to Roy's truck and handed the overnight bag to him. It was small and very light.

Roy said, "It's so light it could blow out of the bed of the truck so I'll just put it in this cooler. It will be kind of crowded up front."

Linda said, "That's O. K."

Roy was also looking forward to the chance to be close.

At that instant, Roy shouted! "***Linda! Get in the back of the truck!! Now!!***"

Linda had just laid her purse on the seat of the truck. She turned quickly and looked at Roy in wide-eyed amazement.

Roy shouted again, "***Now! Now!!***"

She started to move even before she saw the huge wall of water roaring toward them. By then she could hear it, a loud, gushing, splashing sound. Combined with the sight of that terrible behemoth bearing down upon them, it was terrifying.

She scrambled and tried to get up over the side of the truck bed, but she slipped back. Roy leaped behind her and grabbed her. With one hand at her waist, and one hand on her butt, he literally threw her into the truck. Almost in the same motion he vaulted in behind her. Almost landing on top of her as she scrambled to get up.

They got up together, holding on to each other just as the great wall of water slammed in to the side of the truck. The force of the impact almost knocked them off their feet, and scooted the pickup all the way across the blacktop road. It stopped at the edge of the blacktop when the tires hit the mud at the side of the road.

They both looked up just in time to see the Escort roll over and disappear under the muddy water.

Linda emitted a soft, anguished cry and buried her face in Roy's shoulder. In a few seconds she raised her head and looked again at the place where her car had been. There was nothing but the angry hiss and gurgle of the tumultuous torrent as it swirled around the pickup and the Cyprus trees at the side of the road.

She was trembling and Roy held her tight. Again she put her face against Roy's shoulder.

They stood that way for some time. In a little while she looked up at Roy. It touched Roy deeply to see the tears in her beautiful brown eyes, but he was silent. It was Linda who spoke between sobs, "Everything I owned was in that car. I sold everything else before I left. Now I have nothing."

"It will be all right, Linda. It'll be O.K." Roy soothed, "I'm just glad I got you in this pickup before that hit us. I'm glad I've still got you."

Roy didn't know what to do. He was content to just hold her as long as she needed him. He marveled at the pleasure it gave him to hold her, even under such depressing and distracting circumstances. He could smell her hair and feel her hot tears and her warm cheek against his neck.

They stood that way for what seemed like a long time. Roy knew when the tears stopped flowing, but he stayed that way. He was leaning against the cab, and Linda leaned against him.

Slowly Linda relaxed and leaned back to look into Roy's face. Her eyes were red and her cheeks were tear streaked. She said, "Roy, I don't know what I would do if you didn't keep showing up and helping me with every problem. I'm very grateful."

She was still in Roy's arms. She backed away a little more and looked around. The sun peeked through for just a moment.

They both surveyed their situation.

In every direction they could see nothing but the swirling, muddy, swiftly moving river water.

No more the road. It was under five feet of that angry, rising water. There was a lot less of the Cyprus trees showing, and they were swaying in the strong current.

Chapter 12

Saturday Noon

She melted back into Roy's arms and with her head bowed down, she said softly, "Roy, I'm scared."

Her hair tickled Roy's nose as he gently ran his fingers through it. She had left it loose this morning and it was luxurious. Roy loved the way it smelled. Unconsciously, his other hand moved slowly up and down her back, as he said, "Linda, I'm scared too. This is a pretty serious situation. But it's not hopeless. Probably, there will be someone along in a boat to pick us up in a little while."

Roy didn't really believe that would happen. Who would even know they were out there and as wild as this current was at this time, it would be pretty risky for any one in a boat. But he didn't put his thoughts into words.

Even with the distraction of Linda's delightful curves molded against him, Roy's mind was forming a plan. He regretted having to break the spell. They both felt secure in the touch of the other.

"Linda, we've got to be ready. I think our situation is deteriorating fast." Roy said,

He could see the water had risen as much as six inches since that initial crushing blow when the Escort was pushed over and swallowed by the roiling water, and the pickup was violently shoved to the other side of the road, where it sat now, tilted heavily to the left. The big cooler was floating and another four or five inches would allow it to float away on the raging current. Roy also realized that they were standing in several inches of water in the truck bed. Thank goodness, the water was warm. His boots were full.

Slowly he released Linda and told her to lean against the back of the cab for balance on the tilting floor, while he took off the boots.

Linda watched with that worried frown that Roy thought was so pretty on her face. Roy dropped the boots in the corner of the bed where the water was the shallowest. He took off his socks and dropped them in the corner with the boots. Then he took off his shirt and started to throw it in the corner too; he stopped, obviously in deep thought. He turned and dragged the large cooler to him and released both latches and opened the lid and took inventory of the contents.

There were 7- 20 oz. bottles of Pepsi, 2 packages of snack crackers, the small "Emergency Kit" that Linda had handed him, his poncho, and the large package that Mrs. Olson had put in the cooler when he left. All of this did not cover the bottom of the big cooler.

He opened the package. It was a heavy paper sack. Inside was a large zip lock bag which encased another zip lock bag nearly bursting with oatmeal cookies--with raisins, Roy's favorite. That dear lady had double bagged them. All that was left was Linda's small overnight bag. Roy dropped his shirt in the cooler. That left him with just a tee shirt and jeans. He turned to Linda who had been watching silently. She was very close and very beautiful. She gave Roy a small inquisitive smile, and said, "The water is getting deeper, isn't it?"

Roy looked at his watch and said, "I estimate in two hours or less this truck will be totally under, if the force of the current doesn't push it over sooner. We need to have a plan to follow when that happens."

Linda said, looking at the distant hills, "I don't think I can swim that far."

Roy reached for her hand, which she gave willingly, and said quietly, " I don't think either one of us can, in water as turbulent as this. I think our best bet will be to not fight the current but just ride it. The current may carry us to a point close to land or a building where we may want to try to swim for it, but it will have to be close."

She stepped close and put her arms around him. "I'm still scared," she said, " but I believe we'll get through it, together."

Roy pulled her closer and she looked up at him.

The kiss was mutual. They both participated. It was a deliberate meaningful act of respect and genuine affection. It was a definite statement. It wasn't quick, as you might expect of a first kiss, but a lingering, emotional pleasure for both of them.

He put both of his hands on her shoulders and looked deep into her eyes, and said, "I don't want to scare you but this is going to be pretty rough, Linda. Here is what I think we should do."

"In less than an hour this pickup is going to go over and we'll be in the water. This big cooler will keep us both afloat. There is a strong handle on each end. You get a firm grip on one end and I'll grab the other. The current will control where we go. We just have to hope it takes us to safety somewhere downstream from here."

"Now here is another thing. Downstream from this point, according to the map, there is very little population. It's highly unlikely that we will even see anyone. We are a mile and a half from either shore so they probably won't see us."

Linda said, "With this rain and fog and haze I really can't see either shore clearly enough to know if there is another car or truck on the road."

Roy said, "That's right, our prospects of being discovered are very slim. I think probably no one knows we are here, so there won't be a search and rescue attempt made until our vehicles are discovered, which could take days. We could be in the water a long time."

"Mrs. Olson, my recent landlady, gave me this big package of oatmeal cookies with raisins, and we haven't eaten since breakfast. So I suggest we both eat two or three of them to give us strength. It may be a long haul."

With that he reached into the cooler and picked up the cookies. He carefully unzipped both bags and offered them to Linda. Without a word she reached in and took one. Roy took a cookie and opened one of the bottles of warm Pepsi and handed it to Linda. She held the remains of her cookie in her left hand and took the bottle in the other hand. She took a big drink of the Pepsi. They passed the bottle back and forth and each ate two more of the oatmeal cookies. They each offered the last drink of Pepsi to the other, and Roy finally swallowed the last of the drink. He capped the bottle and put it back in the cooler.

They had been sitting on the edge of the truck bed on the high side of the pickup. Roy noticed the low side was just an inch or two above the swirling water, and their feet were in the water now. When they had sat down on the edge of the pickup bed, their feet were just clear of the water. The tilt was steeper now. The wheels were sinking deeper into the mud. He stood up and looked around in all directions. Those friendly Cyprus trees were all that was to be seen, except the muddy water. He could see the levee to the west and the hills to the east, but it was so foggy and misty across the water he would not have been able to see a vehicle even if there had been one there. He pulled the floating cooler over and again surveyed the contents. Everything in the cooler did not cover the bottom even with Linda's emergency kit. In other words it was practicaly empty.

Roy looked at Linda, and she said, "I know, this shirt will have to go."

Roy said, "I want to put it in this cooler. You may need it later. It would be best if you took the shoes off too."

Linda started to unbutton the shirt.

Roy thought, "I've really never seen her but once without that big shirt." He was thinking about last night at the restaurant when he had held the door open for her. "She certainly was a knockout last night," he said to himself.

She opened the shirt and slid it off her shoulders. Roy just stared. She was still a knockout.

When she handed him the shirt, Roy again took her hand; she met him halfway. He dropped the shirt into the cooler and turned back to her. Their second kiss was more emotionally packed than the first. When they separated this time, it was Linda who spoke. "We will make it through this, Roy. We must! We have to! There's so much more to live for now."

Roy smothered any other words with another hungry kiss.

They felt the pickup shift beneath them.

Roy quickly grabbed the cooler and set it up on top of the cab. He firmly fastened both latches. This was their lifeline.

Linda kicked off both shoes and threw them in the corner with Roy's boots.

They climbed up onto the top of the cab. They sat down side by side on the big cooler. The water was spilling over the low side of the pickup bed now. The truck had settled deeper into the mud. The tilt was steeper and the angle at which the truck was sitting was becoming more precarious with each slight shift of the wheels in the mud. The relentless current kept increasing pressure against the side of the truck as the water level rose, driving the wheels further into the mud and having a compounding effect.

Roy looked at his watch. "It's ten minutes 'till one," he said, as rain started to fall again. "Thank goodness it's warm. There's not much use in wishing we had shelter from the rain 'cause I think we'll be wet in just a few minutes." He put his arm around Linda's shoulders. After Linda had taken off the oversized shirt, she felt somewhat exposed, but to the sun. She certainly was not cold even in the rain. She still had on the short-sleeved, white cotton blouse she had put on this morning. The weather had been excessively hot for several days. She was thankful the water she would soon be immersed in was almost as warm as bathwater.

Linda looked at Roy and said, "I'm not as scared as I was. I just know we'll make it."

Roy hugged her close and smiled. "I know we'll make it too. Like you said, we have a lot more to live for now." He kissed her cheek, and said, " It's going to be rough but together we will come out O.K."

They sat in silence for a few minutes feeling the warm rain on their bare heads and on their shoulders, both apparently in deep thought.

Linda stirred as if to speak, but Roy spoke first. He slowly and solemnly said, "Linda, I know this may sound really crazy. ---I just met you and learned your name today, ----- but when this is over --- and we are O.K. · · I don't want us ---- to be over. --- Maybe I've lost my mind, but, Linda, ---- I've never felt more sane."

Linda put a soft hand on his chest and said, "I hope you are not crazy, Roy, because if you are crazy---- I am too. ----I don't want us to be over ----- I ---I think maybe--- we needed each other ----- before we ever met."

The rain pelted down on them as they sat there on the cooler in each other's arms oblivious to the rain. The kiss they shared could not have been more meaningful in the most romantic situation imaginable.

They sat there and held each other for what seemed like a long time. Linda could feel Roy's strong steady heartbeat and Roy had his chin on top of her head. The rain ran down off Roy's face onto the top of her head.

Chapter 13

The Pickup Goes Under

They were both soaked. Linda's beautiful hair was wet. But she had tied it into a ponytail using a small elastic band from her emergency kit in the cooler.

Wet or dry, Roy thought, she is still beautiful.

It had not occurred to either one of them to complain. They were so content, so confident in their feelings for each other. They were actually happy just to be together no matter what the circumstance.

Their euphoria was shattered by the sudden lurching of the pickup! ***This was it! It was going to go over this time!***

Roy gave Linda one quick squeeze and said, "Grab the handle and hang on tight, honey. We're going over this time!"

And they slid into the muddy swirling water.

The buoyancy of the big cooler was more than adequate to keep them afloat. When they first went into the water the current whirled them around so they were floating backward. After a few tries they found they could each hold their respective handle with one hand and put their other hand and forearm on top of the cooler. With a couple of kicks they had the cooler turned around and could now see where they were going.

They didn't talk much at first. They were too engrossed in navigating their strange craft. In a short while they became comfortable with the way they could control their direction as long as it was down stream. They could maneuver side to side and increase their forward speed with a few strong kicks, and Roy found he could hold the handle with one hand and stroke with the other, thereby further increasing their maneuverability. But their course was steady downstream. There was no reason to fight the current until they had a target. All they could see downstream was water. They turned around once to look back. They were surprised at how far they had drifted. Those Cyprus trees that had kept them company that early afternoon were almost out of sight. Now and then a small treetop would show above the surface, and once, about a mile away, a grove of larger trees appeared, but mostly it was just muddy water.

Roy wasn't sure what time it was when they had slid into the water because he hadn't looked at his watch but he thought darkness would come in two or three hours. He looked at his watch and it was still running. It was 5:45. He looked back again to see how far away the Cyprus trees were. They were out of sight. He made some mental calculations. Then he said to Linda,

"We must be drifting at a rate of about two, or maybe three miles per hour. If we went into the water at 2:30, just a guess, it looks like we've been drifting for a little over three hours. That would put us between 6 and 9 miles from where our vehicles went under. We don't know how long this valley is, but at some point this water will merge again with the main channel. We don't want to be in the water when that happens. That current will be vicious. I would sure like to find an old building or some place we could land before dark. It may be a rough night if we don't."

Linda replied, "I hope so to, but if we don't we'll just have to float like this. We'll make it, Roy. I'm not really very tired. We'll be all right."

Roy said, "Linda, you certainly are a treasure. I don't know what I'd do if you were really scared and in a panic. I would definitely want to help you and comfort you but I don't know how I could, under these conditions."

Linda took her right hand off of the cooler and put it on Roy's shoulder and said, " I believe in you, Roy, and together we'll be all right."

At risk of capsizing their unstable craft, Roy leaned over and kissed her.

A minute or so later, Linda said, " What is that, over there?" Roy said, "Over where?"

Linda pointed to Roy's right and slightly behind them.

"There," she said.

Roy twisted around and spotted the object, about 30 yards away.

"I think I'll pull us over there and we'll have a look," he said, and he started kicking and stroking.

He soon noticed Linda was kicking too. They intercepted the object quickly and kept pace with it easily; in fact, they circled it twice as they studied it. Roy said, "I think it's a garage door or a barn door. It's probably floated off of the track from some building. It's almost new. It has been painted recently, new wood, it's solid."

They had noticed a considerable amount of debris floating along all afternoon but this was the largest piece of anything they had seen. Roy said, "It looks to be about 8 or 9 feet square. It's for sure a door, a sliding door, part of the rolling mechanism is still on this side. I've got an idea. It's floating high in the water. It may work as a raft. Let's try something, Linda."

"Try what?" she asked.

Roy had a hold on the door with one hand and the cooler with the other. He said, "Linda, take hold of this door with both hands and let me have the cooler."

She did as instructed.

"Now," Roy explained, "I'm going to try to shove this cooler up onto the door to see how it will ride. This may be our safe haven for the night."

Then Roy took a firm hold on the door with his left hand and got his right hand behind and slightly under the cooler and then gave a mighty shove. It worked and the cooler slid up onto the door.

They both held onto the door now; it easily kept them afloat. Roy worked his way around to the opposite side of the door from Linda. " Now, Linda," he said, "try to heave yourself up onto the door, but just lay flat, don't try to stand up and try to stay as near the middle as you can. I'll hold this side to try to keep it level."

Linda understood immediately. She put both hands flat on the boards and gave a sudden push to propel herself up. Her torso landed on the boards in two or three inches of the muddy water. She gave another heave and that brought her legs aboard. She lay on her stomach with her chin in her hands to keep her face out of the water. The cooler sat on her right almost ready to float in the shallow water that now covered the door.

Roy released his hold on the door long enough to applaud her performance.

"Now you can rest a while and when I get tired we can trade places." He didn't really think it would work very well with his extra weight but he didn't put his thoughts into words. "If you want to take a nap, you can roll over to your back."

Linda said, "I don't think I'm ready for a nap yet, but I will rest so I can relieve you when you get tired."

Roy just smiled. " What a girl," he said to himself.

Chapter 14

Saturday, 6 P.M. In The Water

They drifted along like this for the next thirty minutes or so. Their conversation was small talk about the debris that floated on the surface, sometimes close and sometimes distant. There were tree limbs, old boards, new boards, cans and bottles of all descriptions, everything the river could gather up on its rampage across two states.

Once a flock of geese flew over and settled on the water about a hundred yards ahead of them.

Roy said very quietly, "Lay real still and they may let us drift right through them."

The geese were drifting too so it took several minutes to overtake them. Roy was kicking quietly and pushing the door slowly toward them. When they were almost close enough for Linda to touch the nearest one, it paddled to the side and let them pass. Soon there were geese all around them.

They drifted with the flock for a little while. The geese were communicating with a series of low, quiet, honk like sounds. Then at some indiscernible signal, they skittered across the water and became airborne toward the south.

Roy said, "We may meet them again later."

Linda said, "That was a thrill. They were all around. They must have thought we were just driftwood. We were so close I could see their eyes but I didn't want to turn my head or move."

Roy replied, "Any movement would have alarmed them and they would have left in a flash. I think they just decided to go someplace else. After all, it's kind of boring here. Don't you think?"

Linda rolled to her side laughing. The sudden movement caused the raft to tilt and she had to grab the cooler. It wouldn't have gotten away but she instinctively grabbed the handle.

Still laughing, she said, "This day has been anything but boring."

More soberly she added, "Roy, in some ways this has been a very wonderful day and in some ways a terrible frightening day. I think in the long run I will say it has been a uniquely wonderful day, but never boring."

"I just hope we can find someplace more substantial than this raft to spend the night," Roy said, hopefully.

Linda said, "You must be tired. Let's trade places for a while."

Roy thought, "That may be a good idea. I'll just try it to see if I can ride on it without sinking it."

To Linda's surprise, Roy said, "O.K. we'll try it for a few minutes."

Linda immediately slid back off of the board into the water beside Roy. They each held on to the door with one hand and hugged each other with their free arms. They enjoyed another kiss, and Linda said, "Hop on, I'll drive. I want you to rest a little."

Roy did as he had instructed Linda. When she was on the other side to counterbalance his weight, he heaved himself up onto the boards. His extra weight caused the raft to sink a little lower into the water than Linda had, but if they became desperate they could alternate rest periods.

Up on the board Roy was out of the water a few inches higher and it gave him a better look at the surroundings. They didn't know how deep the water was, but he could see small treetops now and then and only guess at how tall the trees might be.

He could see the levee on the west side of the valley and the hills on the east side. He could see that the levee made a bend to the east, downstream about a mile. He wondered what was around that bend.

It seemed that the current had slowed a little.

Roy said, "When we get around that bend we'll switch places again. How are you doing?"

Linda answered, "I'm fine. We can go a long time like this. I'll watch while you rest and you watch while I rest."

As they came around the bend a little later, Roy could see a row of small treetops, with just a foot or so sticking out of the water. On the end of the row nearest the hills on the east, there stood a large tree. From this distance it appeared to be a very large tree. It looked like the branches extended far out from the trunk. It was by far the largest tree they had seen on their journey.

They were getting closer now and the current was carrying them straight toward the big tree, "a sycamore tree," Roy thought.

At this point the valley had narrowed to maybe a little over two miles. The big sycamore tree was a half or three quarters of a mile from the hills on the east.

The current seemed to have bounced off of the levee on the west side when it hit the big bend, and now was flowing in a southeasterly direction, toward the large tree.

As they drew closer, Roy could see they were going to have to do some kicking and stroking if they were going to miss that tree. But wait! Roy carefully raised up for a better look.

Linda said, "What's wrong Roy? Is there a problem?"

"We're on a collision course with that tree, unless we push our raft off course enough to get around it. But I want to look at it a little closer. I have an idea that might work."

"What? Roy, tell me!"

"When we get a little closer, I'll be able to make a better judgment of the plan. But here it is. Do you see those two huge limbs that point out toward the south?"

"Yes, I see them," she said.

" I think they come out of the main trunk of the tree at no more than a foot under the surface of the water, and they are under water for about four or five feet, and then they are almost horizontal. If my estimates of feet and inches are close enough, we may be able to maneuver this door around and slide it up on those two big limbs. At a point fifteen feet from the trunk they are nearly horizontal and about seven or eight feet apart, and eighteen inches or two feet out of the water. If we aim it and time it right, the current will swing it around and lodge it against this closer limb. Then I will try to push and pull it up onto the two limbs. That should make a good solid platform."

"Let's switch places now," he said, as he slid back into the water. Linda quickly climbed back onto the raft.

She said, "I see what you have in mind, but what if we lose the cooler?"

"We must keep control of the cooler somehow. We're close enough now I can see the plan has a very good chance of working."

"Do you want to try it, Linda? Daylight will be gone in another hour and I don't like the prospects of floating like this in the dark."

"Let's do it, Roy. I think it's a good idea. I'll try to keep control of the cooler so you can concentrate on the door."

"That's great, Linda. I believe we can do it. We're getting close now. Do you see that limb that is pointing out directly at us? About three feet out of the water?"

"Yes! I see the one you mean."

"O.K.! When we float under that limb, stand up quickly and grab it with one hand and hang on to the cooler with other. If you can, throw one leg over the limb and straddle it. But hang on to the cooler. With no weight on the door it will float higher in the water and scoot farther up on the limbs. It's going to work, Linda! I know it is!"

"Things are going to happen fast in about two minutes." The raft moved steadily, unerringly, toward the large tree trunk. Roy was kicking and stroking first one way and then the other, guiding the door into position. The part of the rolling mechanism that was still on the door would work to advantage, if Roy could get it to catch on the massive tree trunk.

Linda moved into a crouching position and said, "Tell me when, Roy." She was facing Roy and couldn't see how close they were to the trunk.

Roy said, "As soon as you feel it bump the tree, make your move, it's close. Be ready y y yyy. Now!"

Linda quickly stood up in the center of the raft with the handle of the cooler in her left hand. She did a half twist and threw her right leg and her right arm over the big limb. She was secure on the limb and the cooler handle was gripped tight in her left fist.

Roy shouted, "Perfect! Linda. Just hang on," as she rolled up on top of the limb.

With the impact of the door against the tree Roy moved fast. He shoved hard to push the door toward the two limbs. The door spun around and lined up on the two limbs just a little off center. He braced his feet against the huge limb under the door and pulled it back a few inches, and then he braced his feet against the trunk and with one mighty heave he pushed the door up onto the two limbs until the lower end of the door was no longer in the water. He pushed again and that brought the lower end of the door out of the water about eight inches. The upper, outermost end of the door was only a little higher than the lower end, not level but quite satisfactory

Linda couldn't clap and maintain her hold on the cooler but she cheered heartily from her perch.

"Way to go, Roy! That looks really solid. It worked just like you thought it would. That's great!"

Roy swam two or three strokes to her and said, "I'll take the cooler and put it on our deck, or porch, or living room, or whatever we choose to call it."

She released her end as Roy took hold of the other end and started toward their platform. Roy pushed it upon the deck and turned to help Linda. She was already in the water and right behind him. It was easy to climb onto the platform by putting one foot on a smaller limb that grew horizontally out of one of the larger limbs at a point about six inches under water.

Roy stayed in the water until Linda had climbed upon their deck. He was right behind her. They stood up together and immediately came into each other's arms.

Nothing was said for several seconds and then they both started talking at once.

Linda said, "This is certainly better than floating all night in the dark."

Roy said, "You probably won't hear any complaints in the morning that the beds were too soft."

They both laughed. They were so relieved that the plan actually did work. They realized they were not, by any stretch of the imagination, out of danger. They did not have a plan beyond just getting through the night as comfortably as possible.

All afternoon it had been raining intermittently, sometimes very lightly, sometimes it was a downpour, sometimes it would stop completely for a few minutes. It was raining when they drifted with the geese but it had stopped when they found the door. They almost didn't notice whether it was or was not raining. It didn't make any difference. They were wet when they slid into the water and they stayed wet.

At the moment they climbed onto the platform it was raining and now it had stopped. That's the way it had been all afternoon. The foliage overhead dripped almost as if it were raining. The tree towered high above them, at least fifty or sixty feet. Roy figured their perch must be twenty- five feet or more above ground. It was a great tree, probably well over one hundred years old. It made a welcome temporary home for these weary travelers.

They didn't realize how weary they were until they sat down on the cooler and they were hungry.

They said, almost simultaneously, "It would sure be nice to have a shower." They both laughed giddily at how ridiculous that sounded. "All day in the water and we want a shower. What we need is some soap. We have a never ending shower."

"And some big fluffy bath towels would be nice," said Linda. "Oh! Wait! I think I can solve the soap problem! Let me in that cooler."

They got up off of the cooler and Roy opened it. Linda grabbed her Emergency Kit and dug into it. "Oh darn, maybe I didn't put it in. Oh, yes! Here it is." She withdrew a partially used bar of well wrapped motel soap.

She explained, "I really liked the way this soap smelled so I wrapped it and put it in my Emergency Kit. Could this be called an Emergency?"

Roy grabbed her impulsively and kissed her then backed away and kissed her again. Both kisses were returned with interest.

Chapter 15

Saturday Almost Dark

All afternoon they had been in the water, over five and one half-hours. And now, to stand on their feet, their legs felt rubbery and unstable, but it felt good to be upright. They were weaker and more tired than they thought. The tension and exertion had exhausted them.

They had neither one eaten anything except the three oatmeal cookies they had eaten sometime around one o- clock. They had both had a light breakfast. In fact, sometime during the afternoon when the subject of food came up, Linda discovered that they had both ordered " Egg McMuffin" and coffee from the same drive up window about fifteen minutes apart.

At that moment there was no rain.

Roy said, "We'll have to wait for rain to use the soap." They were sure they wouldn't have to wait long.

"It will be getting pretty dark in about an hour," Roy said. "We should eat soon. We don't have much to eat, so I think we should ration it out until our prospects of getting help look a little better. What do you think, Linda?"

Linda said apologetically, "I don't have anything to contribute to the groceries so I shouldn't take a ration."

Roy turned sharply and grabbed Linda's upper arms just below the shoulders. He kissed her quickly and said, "Linda, please don't ever talk that way again. Whatever is in that cooler is ours to share. I want it to always be that way. I want us to share our lives."

Tears started to form in Linda's eyes. "I want that too, Roy. I do want us to share our lives."

Roy held her at arms length and looked into her eyes at the tears. "Then, Linda, we won't ever have to have this conversation again. It is settled between us." And he kissed the tears away.

The sky had darkened and it started to rain again, lightly at first, and then suddenly very hard. The hard rain hitting the leaves of the big sycamore tree made so much noise they had to almost shout to be heard. Roy said, "Let's use some of that soap right now. We have an automatic shower. We just can't turn it off."

Roy peeled off his tee shirt and held it out between his hands and forearms so the rain was hitting it fully. In a few seconds he would wring it out and then repeat the process. Linda watched and admired Roy's muscular arms and shoulders for just a moment and that interesting chest hair that traveled down and disappeared behind his belt. She then shyly unbuttoned her blouse. It had been pretty and white this morning but the muddy water had turned it a muddy tan. She started to do as Roy had done with his tee shirt but Roy had finished with his tee shirt and draped it over a convenient limb over his head. He reached for Linda's blouse. He rinsed it thoroughly and hung it up beside his tee shirt. When he turned back, Linda had slipped off her bra and was rinsing it vigorously.

Roy didn't even try to not look. He stepped closer and without touching her, he said, "Linda, you are beautiful." He took the bra from her hand and hung it over the limb. He hooked a couple of the hooks so it couldn't fall off. He turned back to her and repeated, "You are so beautiful." He didn't trust himself to hold her like he had when they were dressed. He didn't want to offend her. He stood awkwardly with his hands down at his sides.

The rain still poured down relentlessly.

Linda said, "Roy, I don't want you to think that I'm shameless, but somehow with you, I think it's all right."

She took two steps and went into his arms as the rain beat down on them harder than ever. She had loosened her hair when the rain started and now Roy slid his left hand up her naked back and ran his fingers through her wet hair. He brought his right hand up to cup her full breast. The nipple was rigid. They kissed long and deeply and Roy's desire was very strong. Linda's was too but they both realized the futility of their situation.

With considerable frustration they repressed and subdued their intense desire.

Finally, Roy said, regretfully, "I'm truly sorry, Linda, but I know this is not the time or place."

Linda hugged him tightly, her bare breasts pressed against his naked chest. And she said, tremulously, "I know, Roy. I'm sorry too, but you are right. The right time will be soon, very soon I hope."

They ended their embrace slowly, and Roy said, "Maybe we should use the soap now, while there is still a lot of rain to rinse in. Thank God it's warm."

Linda agreed, "It's almost dark so we better hurry."

"Yeah, and we better eat too. We can put my big poncho over our heads to keep the rain off of our cookies."

Linda unwrapped the soap and handed it to Roy. He had an instant lather and handed it back to Linda. He rubbed the lather over his neck and chest and then his face and even his hair. He could see Linda was doing much the same thing as he had done. He really wanted to offer to wash Linda's back but he knew the contact would just rekindle the flames of desire that they had just tried to extinguish.

The rain washed the soap out of his hair and into his eyes. He was so captivated with Linda's beauty he didn't want to close his eyes, but he warned Linda about getting soap in her eyes.

"Too late," she said, I already have soap in my eyes."

Linda laid the soap on the cooler and they both stood there with their faces upturned and their arms outstretched to let the rain finish their meager, inadequate baths.

It didn't take long for the rain to remove all traces of the soap. The bath, such as it was, made them feel better and hungrier.

Roy opened the cooler and took out the large poncho. It was six feet wide and nine feet long with a slot in the middle for the wearer to put his head through plus a hood to put over his head. This was a very effective piece of gear for one large person in a rainstorm. But there were two people so they both huddled under it. The rain still fell heavily as they used Roy's shirt to dry their faces and hands.

Then Roy asked Linda to put her large shirt on. He said, "Honey, you are just too distracting like that. I love what I see but I just can't handle that much temptation."

They laughed and Linda kissed him tenderly. She had never felt so much desire, but she knew that this was not the time to say how she felt.

They were actually pretty well protected from the rain, after they got themselves arranged under the poncho. They even had the large cooler under there with them.

Roy opened the lid and got out the snack crackers. He gave one package to Linda and took the other one and started to open it.

Linda said, "Do you want to open both of them?"

"Yeah," Roy said. " I like to alternate them."

Each package had eight smaller individually wrapped packets of six small sandwich crackers with either peanut butter or cheese.

They each chose a packet and Roy opened two bottles of the warm Pepsi.

Food had never tasted so good. They each ate two packets of the sandwich crackers and then they opened the cookies that dear Mrs. Olson had fixed for him. Linda thought they were delicious. They each ate two of them and Roy reached for another one and handed the bag to Linda.

She took another one, and said, "That sure was nice of your landlady to send this big bag of such tasty cookies with you. I want to meet her personally some day and thank her. Maybe she'll let me have the recipe."

Roy said, " I'm sure she won't refuse you. And we will go see her soon. I want to show you off."

He couldn't see her blush. It was getting too dark. Linda said,

"We have to get out of this tree and back to civilization so I can show you off too."

Chapter 16

In The Tree

"I don't know how we will get out of this," Roy said, "but we will. Right now we need to figure out how to get some rest. It's not raining as hard now, but we are seeing flashes of lightening and hearing thunder, so it will probably rain off and on all night. Do you think you can sleep?"

Linda replied, "I don't feel sleepy but I'm very tired. How about you, Roy? Aren't you tired?"

Roy said, "Yes, I'm tired. Let's see if we can find a way to get comfortable under this poncho. The deck will be wet with the rainwater running under us. I'll scoot the cooler up to the high side of our platform right to the edge. Now I'll hang one end of the poncho over the cooler and just over the edge of the platform. That will keep the water from running under us. Will that leave enough poncho for us to get under?"

They sat with their backs against the cooler. Huddled together they were sheltered from the rain but not comfortable. Roy stuck his head out to check on their clothing that was hanging on the limb above them. There was just enough light to see that the three articles appeared to be secure. They were both wearing jeans and that was about all. Linda had her big flannel shirt on, buttoned loosely. Roy reached into the cooler and took out the shirt that they had used as a towel. It was pretty wet, but Roy struggled into it. It was a struggle under the poncho. He left the shirt unbuttoned.

They were both in a strained position. Finally, Roy said, "Linda, turn your back to me and then lay back across my lap. I want to hold you." She twisted around and was soon snuggled in Roy's arms with her head on his chest right under his chin. Her legs were just barely under the poncho, but she didn't care. She felt completely happy and secure.

Roy held her tight and spoke softly in her ear. "Linda, I love you." She turned more toward him and reached up to put her hand behind his head and kissed him passionately. And said,

"I love you too, Roy."

Nothing more was said.

Roy was elated, overjoyed, that they had found each other. He was determined to get them out of this mess, out of this tree and to safety. He didn't know how but he knew he would do it, or die trying.

He felt Linda slowly relax. She was asleep. He softly kissed her on her forehead. She stirred a little and snuggled closer.

Roy sat very still for a long time. He didn't know how long but much later he realized he had gone to sleep too.

The rain had stopped and there was a light breeze blowing through the treetop. For just a minute or less, a pale moon shone through the leaves. Roy looked up to see the blouse and tee shirt fluttering in the breeze. Roy was concerned that the blouse might blow off the limb and be lost but he was reluctant to move and disturb Linda. It was so nice to just sit and hold her but she stirred and suddenly woke up. She pushed back the poncho. In the pale moonlight she quickly saw where she was. She turned back to Roy and hugged him tightly

"Oh, Roy, I'm so glad you're with me," she said fervently. "As terrible as our situation is, I'm happy to be with you."

Roy said, as he stroked her still wet hair, "I enjoyed holding you. I'm really glad to have you. Someday soon we won't be in this situation. It will be wonderful, Linda."

He said, "I think I'd better take our laundry off the line before it blows away."

They both stood up. Roy was stiff and sore from staying so long in one position. He said, as he took their three articles of clothing off the limb, "We must have slept a long time. These things are almost dry. Are you stiff and sore?"

"Only my right hip and leg. I guess that board is pretty hard."

The moon went under again and without that light it was very dark. They stood holding hands for a few seconds while their eyes became accustomed to the darkness. Roy put their shirts in the cooler. He had put the cookies and the snack crackers on the little shelf on one end and he put their still damp clothes on the bottom. The lightening flashed again. It had been pretty quiet for some time but now it was going to start again. The thunder rumbled and then more lightening, more thunder, more lightening.

This was a *Storm* coming! Not just rain like they'd had all day. This was a storm. The wind suddenly picked up and there was a blast of much cooler air. In the flashes of lightning they could see the large tree limbs whipping and thrashing about, overhead.

Roy said, "There may be some hail in this. We'd probably better get under that poncho. That won't be much protection but it's the best we've got. Being near the center of the tree and next to the trunk will give us a better chance of holding onto the poncho in this wind. That big tree trunk will deflect a lot of the wind and hail. We are fortunate to be on the east side of that main trunk. The storm is moving in from the west."

When the lightening flashed, Roy could see Linda's pale face, her eyes were big and frightened.

Roy, having spent most of the last eight years working outside, had a pretty good idea of what to expect from this type of storm. He wanted to shield Linda from all danger. He could see she was really scared. He was scared too. But he knew he would protect her to the best of his ability as long as he had life.

To be up in a tree like this was very dangerous, but that was where they were, and it was better than any available alternative. In other words, they were stuck.

Roy said, "Let's sit on the cooler with our backs to the wind and hold the poncho over our heads. We don't want the cooler to be blown away."

He placed one end of the poncho on the cooler, and they sat on it and drew the rest of the poncho over their heads.

Roy had his left arm over Linda's shoulders while holding the poncho with the other.

Linda was holding on to the poncho with both hands.

Linda had not said anything for several minutes. She finally said, "Roy, I'm so glad you are holding me. I'm scared but with you I'll be all right." And she put her head on his shoulder and let her body melt against him.

Chapter 17

Saturday Night, A Fierce Storm

They had just gotten the poncho firmly in place when the first raindrops hit. The wind was driving the rain hard, almost horizontally through the tree behind them. And then the hail started suddenly as if dumped directly on them from a huge bucket. It pummeled Roy's arms and back through the poncho. One particularly hard gust of wind drove the nickel sized hail horizontally through the tree, blasting them from a different angle, hitting them on the lower back through the poncho. It rattled loudly off the exposed side of the cooler. It was a frightening sound clattering through the tree limbs and on their wooden platform. Roy's arms and shoulders took most of the beating but the way he held the poncho protected their heads.

When the hailstones hit, there was a sting of pain, frightening, but not unbearable. The poncho muffled and softened the impact of the hailstones considerably.

When the sudden gust caused the hailstones to hit them on the lower back, Linda emitted a soft cry of pain, fear, and surprise, but she did not release her hold on the poncho.

Mercifully, the hail did not last long. In less than five minutes the hail dwindled down to just an isolated hailstone or two, or three, rattling through the tree. Then the hail stopped and the rain slackened.

The air had turned much cooler. So they sat on the cooler under the poncho, huddled as close as they could get for warmth. The wind was still blowing and the rain was still falling steadily. Roy could see through the branches. When the lightning flashed there were small whitecaps on the water.

The storm was diminishing, moving on to the southeast. The rain suddenly stopped. In a few minutes the wind calmed and soon was gone.

Linda stirred. " I'm glad that's over," she said. Roy replied, " I'm glad too, honey. Are you hurt or bruised anywhere?"

"Just my lower back and my butt still stings a little but I don't bruise easily. I am O K, but that sure was scary. I was afraid the tree might blow down."

Roy moved his left hand down to gently rub the sore spots .He didn't know if it was doing any good, but she didn't complain and he was certainly enjoying the exploration.

They both noticed when the breeze stopped. The air became warm and humid again. They didn't know what time it was. Roy guessed it could be about three o-clock but it was too dark to see his watch.

He stopped his wandering massage. Linda turned to him in the dark and kissed his neck and then they repositioned themselves and kissed deeply and hungrily

They were both very tired. It had been a nerve wracking and tiring fifteen hours.

Roy laid the poncho down on the deck with about half of it over the cooler. Then he lay down on the poncho on his left side with his back to the cooler and had Linda lay down, close, with her back to him. They were nested like two spoons in a drawer. Then he reached back with his right hand and drew the other half of the poncho over on top of them. He had his left arm under Linda's head and his right arm over her torso. Her left breast snuggled perfectly in his right hand. She was still wearing her large flannel shirt and Roy still had his flannel shirt on. They were a little on the chilly side but under the poncho lying close together they soon became comfortable, as comfortable as was possible lying on the hard board.

They were both exhausted and they both slept almost immediately.

A little later a light rain began to fall, just a soft pattering on the poncho. There was no lightning or thunder this time just the soft warm rain. They stirred and Linda murmured softly, "Roy, love you," and wriggled even closer in his arms. Then she was sound asleep again.

Roy marveled at how she could mold her body so close, so invitingly, as to almost become an extension of his own body. He caressed her breast tenderly and then he was asleep.

They slept soundly. They didn't know when the rain stopped but at some point during the night they had changed positions slightly. Roy started to awaken first. He had turned and now he was almost lying on his back up against the cooler with his right arm over his forehead to keep the poncho out of their faces. Linda had turned over, and now faced Roy with her head just under his chin. Her left leg was over his legs and her left hand had found its way under his shirt to rest possessively across his bare stomach and chest.

Roy was awake now but he didn't move. He just lay there savoring the feeling that this beautiful, loving, young woman seemed to be so content to be there in his arms. As unreasonable as it was, Roy was sure he loved her. He had known love before. He was no adolescent, star struck, impatient kid. He now knew that mature true love at first sight could happen. It had happened to him.

Indisputably!!

He was awed by the fact that the feeling was mutual. She had said she loved him. Somehow, Roy knew he could trust her. He wanted to know, but he didn't care who she was or where she came from. Whatever she was, or whoever she was, Roy knew he loved this woman.

He still had not moved. It was dark under the poncho and very quiet outside.

Without moving Linda very quietly said, "Are you awake, Roy?"

Roy said, "Yes."

Linda said softly, " I've just been lying here listening to your heartbeat and thinking how wonderful it is to be with you. I know we are in a very dangerous and uncertain predicament here, but I also know I love you, and I'll always want to be with you. Whatever happens."

Roy sat up and threw the poncho back and drew her into his arms and tenderly said, "Linda, I've been lying here thinking the same things. We both know we are in a tough spot, but, I too think it is wonderful just being with you. I love you."

They joined in a long, passionate kiss that built their confidence in each other to a new high. Their physical desire was almost out of control. Roy's desire was quite visible in his tight wet jeans.

They breathlessly parted from their highly emotional embrace both realizing again that this was not the right time or place for the consummation of their intense desire. They slowly stood up unwilling to break the spell, but rationality, reluctantly overcame their disappointment.

So intense had been their concentration on each other that they had not realized until now that there was a bright morning sun shining through the sycamore leaves.

It was a beautiful morning, if you looked to the east, but in the west there were more dark storm clouds slowly moving in.

Roy said, " We could sure use a bathroom." Linda agreed wholeheartedly. "I don't think I can hold out much longer."

Roy studied the limb overhead, where he had hung their wet clothes last night. " I think I can hang the poncho over that limb, and we will have two private bathrooms, but no toilet paper."

Linda said, "I think I can solve that problem." She opened the cooler and grabbed her Emergency Kit. She reached into the little side pocket and pulled out a small packet of Kleenex.

Roy flipped the poncho over the limb and let it hang down to the floor. "And now," he said, "you can have your choice. Do you want the northeast bathroom or the southwest bathroom?"

Linda handed Roy some of the Kleenex she had extracted from the packet and stepped daintily around the curtain.

"I like this one," she said, and hurriedly started to undo her jeans.

Roy, on the other side, said, "I'll knock before I come into your bathroom if you'll do the same."

Linda said, "O. K." from her somewhat strained position balancing on the edge of the platform.

Roy quickly unzipped his jeans and urinated loudly over the side. Then he turned around and balanced the same as Linda had to finish his job. He was certainly glad she'd had the Kleenex. When he finished he zipped his pants and buckled his belt and stood looking out through the foliage. He didn't know how to try to signal if a boat came by and it was going to take a long time for this much water to recede. He looked at his watch. It was still running!

They must have slept nearly five hours or more after the storm. He could still feel her soft warm body pressed against him.

"Knock, Knock," he heard. " May I come in?" "Yes," he said happily. " I'll be delighted to see you." He pulled the curtain down and swooped her up into his arms. "See how happy I am? Are you hungry? What would you like for breakfast?"

Linda laughingly said, "Whatever you're having. Just order the same for me." He put her down and kissed her cheek and said, "I think I'll have some cheese and crackers, some peanut butter and crackers, some oatmeal cookies with raisins and about a half of a Pepsi."

"Sounds wonderful," she said. "That sounds like a big breakfast."

Then Roy said, seriously this time, "We can each eat three packets of crackers and three cookies. We should probably share a Pepsi. That will leave us with two full packages of crackers, about a dozen cookies, and three Pepsi Colas. We don't know how long this food will have to last, so it will be best to be conservative. Our worst problem will probably be dehydration."

They ate in silence for a while; then Linda said, " I know you're thinking, Roy. Do you have a plan?" Roy replied, "No, not exactly, but after we eat I'm going to try to climb up in this tree to look around. I don't know what I expect to find but maybe an idea will form when I get a better look at the horizon. I've been watching those clouds in the southwest. They are definitely moving closer. If we are still here tonight we are very apt to have another night like last night."

Linda shuddered, "I hope not. That was scary. The hail and the wind were pretty bad. If it's just rain it can be kind of cozy under that poncho with you. But I know something will have to change soon. I don't know what, but we may have to take some drastic measures."

Roy asked, "Do you have any ideas, Linda? If you do, please tell me?" She answered, "Not really unless a boat would come by or an airplane would fly over. If they did I don't know how we could signal them."

"That's my thinking too, Linda. I just hope I can spot something from high up in the tree."

Chapter 18

Sunday Morning in the Tree

They finished eating and Roy said, "I think it would be a good idea to put our other shirts on and put these shirts in the cooler while they're dry. If that rain does move back in tonight, the dry shirts will feel pretty good under the poncho."

Linda said, "I was just thinking the same thing. The other shirts are still a little wet, but with this sunshine they will dry while we wear them and we will appreciate dry clothes later."

"Do we need private dressing rooms to change?" Roy asked. "I can hang the curtain up again."

Linda blushed and said, "I think we can manage without the curtain," as she opened the cooler. Still blushing, she handed Roy his damp tee shirt. She took her own blouse out of the cooler and shook it out. She did not take the bra out at first but then reached in and brought it out. "This could make the other shirts damp, so I'll leave it out to dry some more and I'll leave the cooler open for a while to let it air out."

She looked up and Roy was just standing there looking at her admiringly. She hung the bra on the open lid of the cooler. She looked back down and started to unbutton the large flannel shirt.

When it was unbuttoned, she let it slide from her shoulders and hung it on the lid next to the bra.

Roy did not move.

She put the blouse on, not yet buttoned.

Roy spoke, "Linda, this is a performance I would like to see repeated every day for the rest of my life."

Roy still had not moved.

Linda slowly buttoned the blouse.

Roy came to her then and took her tenderly in his arms.

"You take my breath away, Linda. I love you."

She reached up and put her hand behind his head and pulled his mouth down to hers. "I love you too, Roy," she whispered. They released each other slowly. They were both breathing heavily.

Roy took off his shirt and hung it on the other end of the cooler lid as Linda had hung hers. He pulled the tee shirt on over his head and for the first time in several minutes he looked at the threatening clouds. He could see they were moving faster than he had originally thought.

He said, "If I'm going to climb this tree I'd better get at it. That rain is going to get here sooner than I expected."

Linda reached for him and gave him a quick hug. "Be careful, Roy. I need you."

That hug and that statement made Roy feel like he could climb Mt. Everest. He reached for the limb where they had hung their clothes. He easily swung himself up onto the limb and from there the next limb above was easy to reach and so on. He was soon high above their platform and he could see the horizon in all directions. In the west he could not see around the big bend but he could see the dark cloud bank that was moving ponderously, slowly toward them.

At this point looking southwest all he could see was the huge levee. But to the southeast was the view that looked like their possible escape route.

He climbed four or five feet higher for a better look.

Linda shouted up through the tree, " Roy, are you alright?"

"I'm fine, honey. I'll be down in just a few minutes."

He studied what he saw, checked his directions, and made some mental calculations and then hurried back down the tree.

Linda rushed to him as soon as his feet hit the deck. He was smiling.

She said, "I know you saw something encouraging. Tell me. Please?"

"Linda, Dear, we are going to leave our home in the tree tomorrow morning rain or shine unless it's raining too hard or too foggy to see. We will have to see the shore to be sure which direction we want to go."

"Oh, tell me what. Tell me how?"

"Look over that way,"(He pointed to the southeast) you can't see anything but the foliage of this tree that we are in, but from up there," (he pointed up) "I could see a spit, a peninsula, sticking far out into the water and it's only about three fourths of a mile downstream. If we take a straight line from here, when we intersect with that point of land we are less than one-quarter mile, maybe four hundred yards from the shoreline. But we won't take a straight line from here. We will start angling toward the east shore as soon as we clear the foliage of this tree. The current has slowed down to almost nothing but what current there is will carry us in that general direction. I'm sure the current will swerve around and get faster as it goes around that point of land, but I don't think we will have any trouble making landfall on that spit. In fact, I expect the water will be shallow when we start getting close. We can wade in."

Linda had watched and listened intently as Roy made his speech. She said, "Why can't we leave now? It sounds like a very good plan?"

She was holding his hands as she asked, "Is it because of the thunder?"

He enfolded her in his arms. "Yes, that's why, honey. I believe this is another storm coming. It would be bad to get caught out in open water if the wind blew as hard as it did last night. I know staying in this tree is less than an ideal situation, but we made it through last night's storm O.K. We'll be safer here than in open water, with only the cooler to hang onto."

They stood in each other's arms as the ominous, dark clouds slowly blotted out the sun that had been shining so cheerfully. The thunder was becoming more frequent and getting closer.

Linda started folding their shirts and laid them in the cooler. She picked up the bra and turned to Roy and asked, "Do you think I should put this on?"

Roy smiled and said, "Only if it makes you feel better."

Linda said, "If the bra was clean, and if I was clean, and if my blouse was clean, maybe I would wear it."

Roy laughed, "I repeat only if it makes you feel better. Maybe we'll both be clean soon and maybe I'll even get a shave."

Linda hugged him and said, "I don't care how long your whiskers get. I'll still love you."

Roy picked up the poncho and hung it over the limb. "This is not so we can have separate bedrooms, it's just to get the wrinkles out of the poncho. We'll miss this clothesline."

Linda hugged him again and laughed. "I like your sense of humor, Roy. It relieves the tension."

Chapter 19

Sunday Noon Sam Burkett's Office

Sunday morning Sam went in to his office as if it had been a weekday. He knew it would be a mad house after the levee broke. He had called in almost half of his crew; the other half had already been working overtime. And he knew Monday, even with a full crew, there would be more to do than they could get done.

" Boys," Sam said, "thanks for coming in today. We really have a big job on our hands and tomorrow will be worse."

Richard spoke up, "That's O. K., Sam. We know how bad it is and we've all got relatives or friends that need help."

"Well, you will be paid overtime but it may be ten days before you get a day off. This flood is far from over," Sam said. "So, Richard, you and Jimmie each take a pickup and patrol the roads both north and south near the backwater. You guys can decide who goes north and who goes south. Keep calling in to let me know where the trouble spots are. And Mose, Andy, and Charlie each take a dump truck and haul sand into Clearcreek and Sydney. The National Guard boys are filling sandbags. They are trying to keep the water out of the business district of both towns. Keep 'em in sand. They'll tell you where to dump it. Those poor folks are trying to save their jobs."

"Bill, you stay in the office with me. We'll probably both be busy on the phone and the radio. Make notes and mark the time when you take a call, ' cause we've got to try to keep the messages in order to be fair to everybody."

"O.K. It is time to get rolling," Sam said and they started filing out the door.

The phone rang as he said, " Everybody be careful." He picked up the phone and said.

"County Road Office, Sam speaking."

He listened a few seconds and said, "Hold it," to the caller.

Then he shouted, "Andy, Mose, Charlie!" while still holding the phone. The men returned, and Sam said, "Take the first two loads to Sydney. This is their Constable and they are needing it bad." He returned to the phone as the men trotted out to their trucks.

"Albert, if I know my men, the first two loads will be there in less than forty five minutes. We'll do our best to deliver all the sand you need. Just tell 'em where to dump it."

"O.K., Sam," Albert said, "thanks a lot. If the water doesn't raise too much more we think we'll be able to keep it out of the mill and the downtown stores. Everybody's working as hard as they can to hold it. If it gets into the mill a lot of jobs will be lost. It could make this town a ghost town."

"Good luck to you folks," Sam said, "and goodbye."

Sam and Bill fielded phone calls and worked the radio almost constantly until about eleven thirty and then there was a lull. Sam said, "People must be gearing down for lunch." They finally had a little time to discuss how they would handle the workload in the afternoon.

Meanwhile, Wilford and Dusty were enjoying a day off. They had slept late Sunday morning because they had both worked full shifts on Friday and Saturday, plus working road patrol until eleven o-clock both nights.

They were fishing buddies and Wilfred had just bought a new boat with several features that were not on the old boat. The main feature they were excited about was the depth finder or fish locator. They were understandably anxious to try it out.

The sun was shining and it was a beautiful morning, but they could see the cloudbank slowly moving in from the west and the forecast was more rain and possible storms in the afternoon.

The two friends were admiring the new boat in Wilford's yard. Wilford said, "I sure would like to get her in the water to try out this depth finder, but it don't make much sense to head up to the lake. It could be storming before we get there."

Dusty said, "Yeah, I know, but I'd sure like to see how good that thing is going to work."

Suddenly, Wilford said, " Hey! What about the backwater? We could go around the barricade and unload right off of road eleven. We can be there in five minutes and try her out for a little while before a storm blows in."

"Hey, yeah! That will be great. We'll know how the bottom looks on both sides of the road even under water and so we'll know if the depth finder is right."

"Let's do it," Wilford said. "I'll run in and tell Judy what we're going to do and I'll tell her to call your wife and we're out of here."

In five minutes they had moved one side of the barricade so they could drive through and then replaced it and drove on over the hill.

Dusty said, as he looked out over the great expanse of water, "There's enough water right here to try out a battleship if it's not too heavy."

In another few minutes they had the trailer turned around and backed down into the water. The boat floated off easily and Wilford said, "I'll just leave the truck set right where it is and when we come back we'll run the boat back on the trailer and be gone before we get wet."

He pulled the boat up along side of the trailer at the edge of the road and they climbed in.

Wilford backed the boat out into deeper water using the electric trolling motor, and then he fired up the forty-horse power gasoline engine. He made a large circle out into the backwater over what they knew to be farm fields. He ran the engine at varying speeds from idle to wide open.

They both had wide smiles on their faces. The boat and engine were both performing beautifully.

Wilford idled the engine down and Dusty said, "Let's try out the depth finder," with the excitement showing in his voice.

"You take her for a spin first," Wilford said. He moved so Dusty could take the wheel.

Dusty gladly took over. He started straight down road eleven at half throttle then slowly moved up to full throttle. " This is great," he yelled over the engine noise. About a half mile out he made a wide right turn and then circled back left to the roadbed again. When he was almost to the road, he cut the throttle and stopped the engine.

"I want to see how that depth finder works," he said.

"When we cross over the road the depth finder should show us a four foot jump and then when we get across to the other side we should see a four foot drop off."

Wilford said, "Hey, that's right; that should be a really good check."

They sat there dead in the water while Wilfred got out the instruction book. They turned on the power and immediately there was a picture on the screen with numbers but they didn't know how to read what they saw. Wilfred read the instruction book and Dusty handled the knobs and buttons.

Soon they had the basics figured out and it showed that they were sitting in water between eleven and a half and twelve feet deep with a flat level bottom.

Dusty said, "That's just what it should read. We know this whole field is level and flat and by my estimate this should be about twelve feet deep right here. Let's go over and cross the road and see what we get." Wilford was at the controls of the trolling motor. He tooled around on a heading to intersect the road.

Dusty was watching the screen. There were a few little blips that they thought may be corn stalks on the bottom as they moved slowly toward where they thought the road was.

Suddenly there was a jump on the screen and there it was. They were directly above the road and the water was seven and one half feet deep.

Wilford grabbed a six and one half foot fishing rod from the rod holder on the side of the boat and thrust it straight down into the water and then leaned over the side to reach down as far as he could into the water. " I touched it!" he cried excitedly. "I touched the blacktop! I know it was blacktop; I could feel it! That thing must be right on the money. It said seven and one half feet and that's exactly where I found it."

"That's great," Dusty said. "Let's run on out to where those Cyprus trees are. There's a culvert under the road there and a small ditch on each side of the road. We'll see what kind of readings we get there."

Wilford turned off the trolling motor and started the big motor. They left the depth finder on and idled their way toward the Cyprus trees. On the way they zig-zagged from one side of the road to the other and watched the screen show that four-foot jump and the four-foot drop off each time they crossed the road.

Dusty was also watching the clouds. They had moved in until they were almost overhead. He said, "We'll have to keep an eye on those clouds." Wilford was watching the depth finder screen but he looked up and said,

"Yeah, we'll watch 'em but we've got rain suits if we need 'em."

They were within twenty yards of the Cyprus trees now, so they turned off the big motor and turned the electric trolling motor on again.

They crossed the road and back again. Dusty said, " We should be over the end of the culvert just about ---Now!"

"That's it," Wilford shouted. "That thing is really accurate."

"This is really great," Dusty said. "When we fish at the old submerged road bed at the lake, we'll know exactly where the old bridge and the culvert is and there are always fish hiding in those places."

"Let's go across again. I think the ditch is a little deeper on that side. It will show that I'll bet."

They drifted across again and sat discussing the merits of this wonderful machine.

Dusty glanced back at the screen.

"Hey! Whoa! Look at that, Will," he cried. "What is that? That's only five or six feet deep! Now it's gone! Am I seeing things? Or is this machine going bad on us already?"

"No, Dusty, I saw it too. Let's go back over that again." He turned around and lined up on the Cyprus trees and moved the boat in that direction.

"There it is," Dusty cried. "Right! Turn hard right!" Wilford turned hard right and immediately cut the motor. The object was right there. Wilford quickly grabbed his fishing rod again and poked it down toward what ever it was. The rod tip made contact at less than six feet. "It made a sound like metal," he said. " It's not wood, it's not concrete, and it wasn't dirt." as he quickly poked it three or four more times. "Now it's gone."

"Let's go over it some more. I think it's a vehicle. Like a car or a pickup."

Wilford started the trolling motor again at its slowest speed. He said, "It can't be a car or a truck. How could it get here?

"Here, Dusty, you take the controls and I'll probe some more."

Dusty turned the boat back toward the spot about forty or fifty feet south and east of the Cyprus trees. When they got to that spot the object showed again. They were going against the slow moving current, so when it appeared on the screen he quickly cut the power to the motor. The boat coasted a little further; then for just a moment it was stopped.

As soon as the object appeared, Wilford started probing. As they coasted over the target he was making contact but by the time they stopped the target was off the screen.

Dusty did not turn the power back on and in a few seconds the current brought them back over the target.

Wilford said, "This is strange. I'm getting two completely different sounds. This sounds like metal. Can you hear it? Now here it's different. Hear that?"

"Yes, I hear it. That is definitely two different sounds. You know what I think, Will?"

"No?"

"I think that's a car down there, on its side. The metal sound is the door and the other sound is the glass."

"My God, Dusty. I think you're right. The sounds are right."

" We better call Sam."

Dusty said, "Let's check it some more first. We'll check it going the other way." He turned the boat around again and got lined up to run parallel with the roadbed.

It didn't show.

"I think I must be too close to the road," he said. He turned the boat around again and estimated the distance from the Cyprus trees and moved toward the imaginary spot. The object came on the screen this time and Wilford resumed probing. The first sound was metal but it was slightly different. The next two probes were the same as he had heard going the other way. Then he made several more probes before it went off of the screen.

"Damn! That is a vehicle down there, a car, a pickup, or a van," Wilford said.

Dusty had kept the motor on and now was circling back. He said, "We'll make one more pass over it for one more look and then we'll have to call Sam."

As they made the circle, Wilford looked at the clouds. "We had better get those rain suits ready. We won't get back to the truck before it starts raining."

They passed over the vehicle again and both watched the screen.

"I'm convinced," Dusty said. "Get out your cell phone and call Sam and we better call the girls too. They'll be worried if we don't."

Sam answered on the third ring, "County road office, Sam speaking."

Chapter 20

Sunday Afternoon in the Tree

Another louder crash of thunder rolled across the hills and the water, and Linda hugged him tighter.

Roy kissed her softly and tenderly and said, "There's more good news. There's an old barn or building of some kind up the hill about two or three hundred yards from the water. When we get there, I think we will have a roof to get under. That should be more comfortable than the poncho, but I think we're stuck here for another night. After this storm passes it will be too late in the day to start. We'll need daylight to see the landmarks."

Linda molded her body close to his and said, "That's O.K., Honey. Where ever you are that's where I'll want to be. I don't care if it's the "Taj Mahal" or under that poncho. We'll be all right if we're together."

Roy's chest swelled with pride and joy at those words. His resolve to love and protect her was growing stronger by the hour.

The thunder was getting closer.

Roy looked at his watch. He thought, could it be this late? The watch was still running. It said twenty after twelve. He remembered when the clouds covered the sun it was almost straight up overhead. The watch must be right.

He was still holding Linda. He said, "It's twelve twenty, Linda. Are you hungry?" She said, against his neck, "A little, but I'm all right. There's not much left to eat. I can wait a while."

Roy gave her a squeeze and said, "I think you're right. We'll eat a little tonight and we'll save some for tomorrow morning before our swim. Right now I think we should prepare for this new storm. Should we put our shirts on again or wait to see if it gets cool?"

Linda said, " Let's put them on now. It is quite a struggle to put them on while we are under the poncho. I think it's already cooler."

Roy said, "I think so too. We better hurry; the rain will be here any minute."

They had barely gotten their shirts on and crawled under the poncho when the rain started again. Not a hard rain, but a soaker. They were sitting on one end of the poncho with the rest of it up over their backs and over their heads and with the front just over the edge of the platform. They were leaning back on the cooler. They could be comfortable that way for a while, but they would soon feel cramped. The exposure and lack of proper nourishment was beginning to take its toll.

Linda was the first to speak, "Roy, we really don't know anything about each other." She said, "Where are you from?"

Roy answered slowly, "Well, most recently from a little town in western Pennsylvania name of Bentlyville. Interstate 70 runs right by there. But originally I am from west Kansas. That's where my folks live. Just outside Goodland. Highway 70 runs right through there too. That's where I was headed when we had this little problem. It turned out to be a quite wonderful problem for me. I'm glad I didn't miss it."

"Roy, you are very sweet, maybe a little demented, but I love you anyway. What line of work were you in?"

"I was a construction worker and heavy equipment mechanic."

"That explains how you are so quick to improvise and solve problems. You always come up with a solution no matter how serious and complex the situation."

"Yeah, one of my solutions landed you in a sycamore tree." She turned quickly and took his face with both hands.

"Roy, it was a great idea. We're doing just fine. We'll be out of this tree tomorrow." She kissed him on the nose and then on the mouth. "It could have been really serious if we had been in the water during that storm."

"There's a lot more to my story," he said. She didn't flinch or tense up. She just waited for him to continue.

"I was married for about three years."

"That doesn't matter to me. As long as you are not married now."

"I'm no longer married. I want to, need to, tell you about it."

Linda just waited for him to continue.

"I was married three years ago on the twenty first of this month to a girl I met in Bentlyville. We went together about six months before we got married. Her name was Mary Ann, and we named our little girl Dorothy Ann. We were the perfect family."

Roy produced a soggy wallet from his hip pocket, and in the dim light under the poncho, he carefully extracted a small photo encased and sealed in plastic.

It was a studio shot of Mary Ann, Dorothy Ann, and Roy, that had been taken on Valentine's Day about a month before the accident.

Linda held the picture over to the edge of the poncho for more light, as Roy said.

"Dorothy Ann was only ten months old when they were both killed in an automobile accident on the twenty first of March." His voice choked and his breath caught in his throat. "That's why I left Bentlyville."

They were both silent for a long time.

Finally, Linda spoke, "I'm very sorry, Roy. You had a beautiful family and I know this is very painful for you." She hugged him tightly.

Roy could not subdue a sob.

Linda said, still hugging him tightly, "Roy, dear, believe me if you can. I think I know how you are suffering."

Roy said, "There is something else I need to tell you." He paused again, to carefully choose his words. "Linda, I honestly believed I would never love another woman. I really never even looked at anyone else until I saw you in the doorway of that restaurant and again at the station when I fixed your tire. Those two incidents started me thinking maybe I could live again. I was really glad to see you standing there beside your car when I came down that hill. I had been afraid I would never see you again."

The rain continued a little harder now.

They sat in each other's arms and were both silent again for a while. Then Linda spoke softly.

"Now, Roy, I want to tell you my story. It, too, is very sad."

"I was born and grew up in Wisconsin. I went to school, high school, and college in my hometown. I had a normal, happy life. I was close to both of my parents. And they were both killed in a plane crash when I was a sophomore in college."

Roy started to comment, but she continued, "There was quite a bit of insurance and other assets. I was financially secure so I finished college just to keep my mind busy."

"After college I took a job in the business office of a retail chain. It was just to keep my mind off of the void in my life. I worked really hard. It helped to get me finally settled down. When I had been there a little over six months, they offered me a transfer to a new office in Litchfield, Ohio. I moved there and really enjoyed my job. After I'd been there three months, I met Jeff. He worked with computers, installations mostly. We went together for a little over six months and got married. We were married about a year and Jeff's company sent him to Spain to set up a new computer system. He was killed by a terrorist bomb in February. That's why I left Litchfield."

Tears streamed down her face as she finished her story. They held each other close in their own private misery that was no longer private but shared. Somehow in the sharing their burdens were lighter.

The rain was steady, the thunder had moved on, and there was very little wind just the steady persistent rain.

"I'm sorry I can't show you a picture. My billfold, with my pictures, was in my purse that I left in the cab of your pickup."

Roy held her close. She said, " Roy, I've been through the same situation you described, I never dated or even looked at another man. I was asked out on dates and the girls at the office tried to include me in at parties and lunches and so forth but I wasn't interested in anyone until you held that door open for me and the next day when you fixed my tire. And I was afraid I would never see you again, too. I was so thankful when I saw it was you stopping behind me."

They were quiet in each other's arms for a long time. Then they both started to speak at the same time; each trying to apologize for unburdening their cares on the other.

Finally it was Linda who said, "The past is gone, Roy dear. Forever. We know it can never be relived. What we have now is a future."

They sat quietly again. There was no noise except the rain now falling lightly on the poncho.

Chapter 21

Sunday Afternoon In Sam's office

As soon as Sam answered the phone, Wilford started talking.

"Sam, I think we got trouble," Sam broke in.

"Where are you, Will?" You're supposed to be off."

Wilford said, "Me and Dusty are down here in the backwater off of road eleven in my new boat, and there's a car about six or eight foot out on the south side of the road in about twelve foot of water."

"Are you sure? How do you know? How in the hell did it get there?"

"We're sure there is something there that's not supposed to be there. We think it's a car or a pickup. We found it with my new depth finder."

"Well, how in the hell did it get there?"

"We don't know, Sam. Maybe it came from the Bridgton side? I just know it had to get there between Friday about three o-clock and the time the levee broke. I drove down this road the last thing I did before I came in at four to start night patrol on Friday night."

Sam said, "I'll call Fred over at Bridgton to see when they blockaded that end. Give me a few minutes and I'll call you back. Are you on your cell phone?"

"Yeah, I'll call Judy while you're calling Fred. It's starting to rain a little here but we'll wait 'til you call back in case you want us to do any more checking. But we know there is something down there."

Wilford made a quick call to his wife and then Dusty called Susie with a short explanation of the situation.

They put on their rain suits as they waited for Sam to call.

The rain was light, but they would have soon been wet without the rain suits. Dusty seemed to be in deep thought as he stared back at the hills where the pickup was parked. He said,

"You know, Will, if someone drove over that hill," he gestured back toward their pickup and boat trailer, "just before we got the barricade up yesterday morning and then stopped here along the road for any reason, to take a leak, or check a tire, or anything, for twenty minutes or so that's about the time the levee broke?"

Will answered, "If that happened they didn't have a chance."

They had drifted seventy-five or a hundred yards away from the Cyprus trees while they were on the phone and talking. The depth finder was still on and working, showing a steady twelve feet deep.

Dusty turned the trolling motor back on low speed and slowly started back toward the Cyprus trees. The phone's buzzer went off in Will's pocket and he answered it immediately,

"This is Will."

Sam said," Will, Fred said that road was barricaded solid at ten o-clock Saturday morning. They had even dumped a big load of sand at the entrance to the bridge behind the barricade. Nobody could've drove through it."

"Well, we've just been talking, Sam, if somebody drove over the hill and down the road just ahead of us before we barricaded the road and they stopped for some reason, they could have been here when the levee broke. They would have been trapped. They wouldn't have had a chance."

"Check again, Will, before I notify the State Police."

" WILL!! There's something else down here. LOOK!" Dusty shouted.

Will was already looking at the screen. " Sam! There is another object down here. It's not more than forty or fifty feet from the other one."

Sam said, "What the hell happened, Will? Do you think it was a wreck?"

" I don't know, Sam. We just know there is something in the water here that's not supposed to be here."

"You think there are two vehicles off the road, in the field, under water?"

" We sure think so, Sam," Will said. " The water over the road is about seven and one half feet deep and out in the field it's nearly twelve feet deep, and the depth finder clearly shows a big chunk of something that's not supposed to be there, in two different places."

"Well, I know you two guys are savvy enough to know when something ain't right," Sam said. "So I'm going to call the State Police and try to get their dive team to come and investigate this. If there has been a wreck there will probably be some bodies and they will know how to handle them."

"We'll just wait here until you talk to the cops. If they come this afternoon we can show them where to dive," Will said. "Call us back after you talk to them, O K?"

Sam said, "Yes, I'll call you as soon as I find out what the state boys are going to do, and, Will, I put you and Dusty on the clock at one o-clock. This is county business and you are on county time so sit tight and I'll call you in just a few minutes."

Wilford clicked his phone off and said, " Hey! Dusty, we're getting paid for this. Sam put us on the clock."

Dusty had a big grin on his face as he said, "This has always been my greatest ambition, to get paid for just setting in a boat." They both laughed and then Dusty got serious. He was looking out over the water at where the two objects were submerged and he said,

"I wonder what happened, Will? Do you think there are people in those vehicles?"

Wilford said, "I think that's probably what they'll find."

Dusty said, "I don't think they'll be in very good shape if they've been in this warm water since yesterday morning."

"If this was a wreck," Wilford speculated, "the people in that vehicle over there," he pointed toward the object farthest from the road. "could have been thrown out and if that happened, the bodies could be miles from here."

Their hypothetical "what if" contemplation of the situation was interrupted by the cell phone.

Wilford answered, "This is Will."

Sam said, " Boys, the State Police can't get a dive team in here until tomorrow morning about ten o-clock or maybe later. It's three thirty now so you guys go ahead with your day off and I'll clock you off at four. You'll probably have to go out with the divers tomorrow to show them where to look."

The rain still fell steadily but they were comfortable in the rain suits so they were in no hurry to load the boat.

Wilford said, "Let's check her out a little more. I almost forgot we were out here to test out this boat and the tackle and the fish locater."

"Yeah, finding those two vehicles, if that's what they are, has sure took the fun out of a boat ride," Dusty said.

"If there are people down there, nobody even knows they are missing. They must have families?"

"Well, we'll find out tomorrow," Will said. "Let's go back over that area again to see if there is anything else."

They ran the boat back and forth in a criss-cross grid pattern over the two objects and well beyond in all directions but they didn't discover anything new.

Finally Will said, "I give up. I can't think about anything but whatever that is down there. We might as well go home. We'll be back tomorrow."

Dusty agreed, "We know the depth finder is working and the boat and engine and trolling motor all work really good, but

I'm like you. This thing is messing up my mind. Let's go home to supper."

Chapter 22

Sunday Night Cold, Restless

Around seven o-clock the rain stopped falling but the leaves still dripped.

Roy said, "We should probably stay under the poncho until the leaves stop dripping or we'll get our shirts as wet as if we stood out in the rain."

In answer to that statement, a brisk breeze sprang up. It quickly had the water shook off of the leaves and they emerged from their shelter under the poncho.

Again there were dark clouds in the west. Linda said,

"I guess that means more rain but maybe we can eat without the poncho over our heads."

Roy said lightly, " Yeah, but we won't be able to witness a beautiful sunset. Linda laughed and said,

We are going to watch a lot of sunsets together, Roy, and sunrises too." She put her arms around his waist and looked up into his face, and said seriously, "That's a promise."

Roy squeezed her tightly and said, "And I intend to hold you to that promise." Their kiss was long and passionate. When they released each other and looked into each other's eyes, they were both confident in the unspoken promise of love to come. They were each so sure of the other they did not question the brevity of their relationship; they did not question their own feelings, or question the feelings of the other. They just knew.

A long, low rumble of distant thunder interrupted their thoughts and Roy spoke, "We should eat now before the rain starts again. With nothing to drink except Pepsi Cola we will dehydrate soon. We could probably catch some rain water for drinking but it would not be clean, after it runs and drips through this tree." Linda said, "A nice cold bottle of water would taste good I'm sure, but I'm O. K. I can hold out. We must be getting some good out of the Pepsi. I'm just thankful for that big cooler and all its contents."

Roy opened the cooler and said, "We'll ration out about a third of the food that's left, and drink one Pepsi then we'll eat and drink all that's left in the morning before we try to reach the spit. It will take a lot of energy and we've been short on nutrition for two days, so we're not as strong as we were when we first went into the water."

Linda put her arms around him and said, " I know you're right, Roy, but I know we'll make it back to civilization, if not tomorrow, then the next day, or the next. But we will make it."

At this same time not more than a mile away across the water to the east and up the hill a little more than a quarter mile, Herman Schultz stepped out of his house to observe the weather. He saw the same lightning and heard the same thunder that Linda and Roy were hearing. He mused to himself,

"This is the most rain that has fallen on this farm in my lifetime." Herman was born and raised on the farm. The original deed was to his great grandfather and had been passed down to his grandfather and then to his father, and now Herman was ready to turn the reins over to his son.

The original home was down the hill through the woods about four hundred yards. It was near the old barn that Roy had seen from high up in the tree.

Herman returned to the house where his wife of fifty-two years was poring over a recipe book. She loved to cook and had borrowed the book from the library. He interrupted her reading to say, "Tildy, after breakfast tomorrow let's take the pickup and drive down to the old barn and look at the water. It's a sight we will probably never see again. That's a big valley. It is twelve miles long and three miles wide in some places. It's full of water that must be thirty feet deep in some spots."

Tildy said, "I know. It's terrible. Some of our neighbors and friends won't have a crop this year, and Willie will only have a crop on our higher ground."

"Maybe we should take some pictures," Herman said.

"I know the water must be high up in that old sycamore and I'd like to have a picture of it. That is where I used to rest my horses when I was a boy, in the shade of that old tree."

It was decided then that they would ride down in the four-wheel drive pickup to where the old house once stood and take a few pictures.

Once again they heard thunder, closer this time.

Roy and Linda had eaten their small supper ravenously. The short rations and the absence of water to drink was weakening them more than they realized.

Roy said, "We can make it through the night, and tomorrow morning, if it's not too foggy or windy, we'll finish off the food we have left and head for land. Right now we'd better get ready for more rain."

Linda said, "I hope its not another storm. I think it's getting cooler. Does that mean more hail?"

"I'm not sure, Roy answered. "I think we are losing some of our ability to resist the cooler temperature. What we have been through in the last thirty-five hours has taken its toll. We haven't really noticed it, but near total exposure during all that time has had its effect on us."

Lightning and thunder were cracking and crashing all around as Roy was arranging the cooler and the poncho. They were still wearing their flannel shirts and it was time to get under the protection of the poncho.

They could hear the rain approaching across the water from the west. There was a little wind just ahead of the rain but it caused no problems and they sat much as they had the night before with their backs against the cooler. Roy had his arm resting on the cooler behind Linda's head. She leaned against him and he leaned his head against hers. They were both exhausted and they slept a short while until a leg cramp woke Roy. Then they laid down the same as they had last night, with Roy on his left side, and Linda on her left side with her back to him. Again Roy had his left arm under Linda's head, and his right arm over her torso, her left breast in his right hand.

Linda wriggled a little closer and said, "I hope we can keep warm tonight, Roy. It hasn't been a problem until tonight, but I'm definitely feeling more sensitive to the air."

Roy said, "I'm sure glad we kept these flannel shirts dry. If they were wet, we would really be uncomfortable. We'll just stay as close as we can to conserve our body heat."

"Close is where I want to be whether we are hot or cold," Linda said, as she turned to face him.

They lay in each other's arms for a little while as the rain fell steadily on the poncho.

They were very tired and soon Roy turned onto his back and Linda lay with her head on his shoulder and her left arm and leg across his body. That is the way they slept for the next three or four hours. After that they slept restlessly and changed positions several times before daylight.

The rain stopped and started intermittently throughout the night.

Chapter 23

Monday Morning Cold And Windy

By morning the rain had stopped. It was definitely cooler and there was a brisk north breeze blowing through the tree.

The clouds were still overhead but there was a narrow band of clear sky in the east. They stood in each other's arms using the poncho as a windbreak and watched the sun come up through the leaves of the sycamore tree.

Linda snuggled closer to Roy and said, "Do you think we should start keeping score?"

Roy looked at her with a puzzled expression. She explained, "About how many sunrises we'll watch together."

"Roy squeezed her tight with both arms, and said," Let's not waste our time and energy keeping score. We'll just be together whether the sun comes up or goes down. Right now I hope it stays out for a while to warm us up. The water will feel cold when we first go in and we've got a long swim ahead of us."

Roy was concerned about hypothermia. Their lack of good nutrition over the last two days would surely affect their stamina in a long physical workout. And he was expecting their swim to shore to be just that.

They were both desperately feeling the need of a good warm bath and a change to warm clean clothes. They were both wearing the same clothes they had put on in the motel on Saturday morning. And they had been in the muddy water or on their cold, wet platform in all kinds of weather ever since.

The sun was a little higher now and the warmth was beginning to filter through the leaves.

Roy said, "Maybe I should put our bathroom partition up again for a little while and then after that we could use your soap and wash our hands in this muddy water before we eat." He laughed."

Linda said, "I agree with all of the above, especially the bathroom part and I would agree to any way to get cleaned up, even just a little and it's our soap, not just mine."

Chapter 24

Monday Morning, Uneasy Before the Swim

Their morning ablutions finished, Roy took the poncho down from the overhead limb and folded it into a neat, compact, bundle. Linda took the rest of their food out of the cooler. She held the crackers and cookies in her hands while Roy placed the poncho in the bottom of the cooler and retrieved the last two bottles of Pepsi.

They sat down on the cooler and quickly devoured everything including the two Pepsis.

Roy stood and took both of Linda's hands in his and looked into her eyes and said,

"Linda, honey, now we are committed. We can't delay. We need water to drink. There is no more food. And the longer we wait to attempt to reach land, the tougher it will be."

"I know, Roy. I expect it to be difficult, but we'll make it. We just won't give up. I'm ready whenever you say it's time to go."

"Linda, you are wonderful. We have to make it. But I don't want you to be surprised. This wind will make it cold when we're wet and we will be swimming against the wind. I don't expect much trouble from the current until we get almost there. But then we may have to fight the wind as well as the current when we get close to the spit."

"Do you feel cold now?" Roy asked.

"Only a little," she said, "but I'll be all right."

"Well, we'd better take these flannel shirts off and put them in the cooler. When we get out of the water we'll be glad they're dry."

Linda opened the cooler and took their light shirts out and started to unbutton her flannel shirt. Roy watched Linda as he unbuttoned his own shirt. They both slid the flannel shirts off at the same time and dropped them into the cooler. They moved toward each other purposefully and into each other's arms. They held each other without speaking for a few moments. Then Linda said, "This is so nice, to be held by you, Roy. I'm so glad we found each other."

Roy's lips found hers for a long and satisfying kiss.

They parted reluctantly, and Linda handed Roy his tee shirt and laid her once white blouse on the cooler while she put her bra on. She said, "If we find any people when we get to shore, I think I'll feel better with this on."

Roy smiled and said, "Only if you feel better."

They hugged again, and then Roy put his tee shirt on.

As Linda buttoned her blouse, Roy fastened the lid securely on the cooler. He noticed the wind had not let up, and he said, "I don't think the sun will be out much longer. I think the clouds will be covering it soon. It may even rain again before we get to land but if it don't get foggy we should be all right."

The sun had warmed the air, somewhat, so the breeze did not have as much effect on their comfort as it had earlier.

Roy took Linda's hands in his again, and said, "Linda, honey, I don't think we will ever forget our first two nights together." They both laughed, and Linda said, "We may not be able to ever convince anyone that we spent our first two nights together in a tree. But, Roy, it's been wonderful. It hasn't been a honeymoon, but we will have one! Very soon."

Roy still held Linda's hands. He looked into her eyes and said, "Are you ready honey?" She nodded soberly.

Roy slid the cooler over to the edge of the platform. He turned and kissed Linda again.

"Here we go. We'll go out of the tree, right through there." He pointed to the north. "Then we'll kick and paddle in that direction. The current will carry us southeast for a while but if we are paddling north it won't carry us past the spit. We should be getting closer to the shore all the time."

Roy stepped down onto the limb under the north side of their platform and eased down into the water. He pulled the cooler into the water and Linda followed him holding on to the opposite end of the cooler. The water felt colder than they had expected and Roy was more concerned about hypothermia. He didn't say anything but he knew they would have to stay aware of that possibility. They pulled their way through the branches and were soon out in the open away from the tree.

Chapter 25

Monday Morning Sam Burkett's Office

Dusty and Wilford reported in at the office at seven thirty Monday morning. Sam told them to take the right rear wheel off of the number 5 dump truck and install a new tire to replace the one that had blown out Friday afternoon. They were also instructed to check all the lights on that truck.

"The state police said they would call to say when they will be here," Sam said. " And then you guys will have to meet them down on Road Eleven and show them where to dive."

Wilford and Dusty went out to the shop to work on the tire. They were apprehensive about seeing the people brought up from the submerged vehicles.

Dusty said, "I didn't sleep much." Wilford said, "Me too, I kept thinking, " what if there was little kids in those cars. I can't figure how those cars got there? It bothered me all night."

"Me too. I'll be glad when it's over," Dusty said.

They became involved in the task and soon it was nine thirty and Sam called them in.

"O.K. boys. They just called, and they said to meet them on Road Eleven down by the water. You can use your own boat if you want to. They'll be there at ten o-clock."

The boat trailer was still hooked up to Wilford's pickup so it was ready to go. They drove directly to Road Eleven and backed down the hill and unloaded the boat. Dusty stayed in the boat while Wilford pulled the trailer up the hill and out of the way so the police would have room to back their trailer down beside them and unload their boat.

By the time Wilford walked back to the boat, the police were backing down the hill and by the time they got their boat in the water, a patrol car pulled up and stopped beside the police pickup.

There were two men in each vehicle. The one driving the patrol car was in uniform. The other three were dressed differently. Two of them were going to be doing the diving; the third would handle the boat and relay the information to the patrol car. There were introductions all around. There was George, Matthew, Bob, and Sarge.

Two of the men started donning their scuba gear, and the third, Mathew, was checking equipment on the boat

Sarge, the patrolman in uniform would stay ashore and relay information to headquarters on the radio.

Matthew seemed to be in charge. He would be the one operating the boat. He told Wilford and Dusty to lead the way.

Wilford headed straight down road Eleven toward the Cyprus trees. The police boat followed in their wake. It was nearly one and one half miles to the trees and about the same distance to the bridge at Bridgton. They arrived at their destination in less than five minutes. The breeze made the water a little choppy but it would cause no trouble unless it became significantly stronger.

Wilford cut the engine and drifted to a stop about fifty feet from where the submerged objects were.

He pointed to the spot where he thought they should make their first dive. Mathew was in control and he maneuvered his boat to the spot.

Wilford shouted, "You should be over it, right there."

Matthew shouted back, "You're right on. I can see it on our screen. We'll dive right here."

Bob was ready and went backward over the side immediately.

Dusty moved their boat over and let it drift up against the Cyprus trees. The wind would hold them in that position without using the trolling motor.

They waited three or four minutes before Bob surfaced right beside his boat.

He pushed up his goggles and spit out his mouthpiece. He stayed in the water but clung to the side of the boat.

"It's a four wheel drive G.M.C. pickup, 2002 or 2003, I think silver. It's muddy down there. It has got 2004 Pennsylvania plates. It has not been wrecked unless all the damage is on the driver's side. It's lying on the driver's side headed toward Bridgton. The door on the driver's side is open and bent back against the left front fender. That is the only visible damage. There are no bodies."

Wilford and Dusty heaved big sighs of relief. They did not want to see any bodies.

Wilford said, "We've still got one to go, keep your fingers crossed."

Matthew relayed the story to Sarge in the patrol car while Bob went back down to double check the license number. He was up again in less than a minute and gave Matthew the number before he was finished with the other information.

When Matthew had completed his transmission, Bob climbed aboard and George was preparing to make the next dive.

Matthew turned to Dusty and Wilford, "O. K., guys, where is the other vehicle?"

"It's about forty feet south, south west of the first one," Dusty said. Wilford nodded his approval.

Matthew headed his craft in that direction.

Dusty yelled, "Bear just a little to the left."

Matthew made the correction, and Dusty said loudly, "That should take you right over it."

In just a few seconds Matthew yelled, " Right again, Mr. Stiles, you are right on. There it is."

Dusty had given his first and last name when they were introduced, but he was surprised to hear himself referred to as Mister.

This time Wilford dropped the bow anchor. There were no trees to drift against but the wind, which was a little stronger and cooler now, blew them around untill they were broadside to the action and held them there.

George was ready and at Matthew's signal he went over the side.

In three minutes he popped up right beside his boat. He did the same as Bob had done. He pushed up the goggles and spit out the mouthpiece.

He said, " It's a ninety eight or a ninety nine Escort. It is a blue four door sitting on all four wheels, no glass is broke, all doors are locked, and the hood is open. The top is dented in a little, but not bad. The passenger side doors are also dented in a little, but not bad. It is headed toward Bridgton. It looks like it is loaded with clothing, 2004 Ohio license plates," and he recited the number." There are no bodies."

There was another huge sigh of relief from Dusty and Wilford.

Matthew recited this information to Sarge. The perplexity and confusion of this situation had them all bewildered.

The dive team had come up with more questions than answers.

Chapter 26

Monday Morning Start The Swim

Roy quickly took bearings from trees and hills to the north and to the east to gage their direction and progress.

He said, "Let's just kick and paddle slow and easy for now and see how our direction works out. The wind may be more of a factor than I expected."

"Do you see the spit I'm talking about? The peninsula?"

Linda answered, "Yes, I think so, the row of small trees way out in the water and then they get bigger toward the shore?"

Roy said, "Yes, that's it." I think the water is shallow far out into the main body. If I'm right we can wade the last few yards. At least it looked that way from high in the tree."

He turned and looked back at the big sycamore. Their progress seemed to be satisfactory. He checked his bearings from the hills and trees. It didn't look like they were as close to the shore as he thought they should be.

Linda looked back too. She studied the tree from the distance for just a moment. Then still looking back at the tree, she said,

"Roy, I guess I'm being foolish but I'm feeling very sentimental about leaving that tree. As scary and uncomfortable as it was, it was wonderful being in your arms, under that poncho. It was scary and it was uncomfortable but it has been like finding something that I had been looking for, for a long time, and I'm so glad I found it. You! From the time you stopped your pickup to help me for the second time, it has been increasingly wonderful."

Roy said, "I was feeling the same way about our tree, Linda. And we will, someday, after the water goes down, come back to visit our tree."

They were both lost in their own thoughts for a few moments, and then Roy said,

"Linda, you mentioned a honeymoon a little while ago. Wouldn't you have to be married before you had a honeymoon?"

Linda said seriously, "You are right, but no one has asked me."

Roy took her hand, which was on top of the cooler, and looked into her eyes and said, "Linda Powers. Will you marry me?"

Linda's eyes filled with tears, and she said, "Yes, Roy dear, a thousand times, Yes!"

Roy moved toward her behind the cooler. Holding the handle with his left hand he drew her close with his right arm. They kissed with as much passion as they could under the circumstances. When they separated, Roy looked at Linda with alarm. Her lips had felt cold, and Roy had felt her shiver.

Hypothermia! Dehydration! Roy didn't know?

"Linda, are you cold? Tell me how you feel."

Linda answered, "Yes, I do feel cold, but I'll be all right."

Roy said, "O.K., but we'll be in the water nearly an hour yet. You be sure to tell me if you start feeling different."

Roy looked around to check their progress. They were not as close to the land as he wanted to be.

"O.K, Linda, let's start kicking and stroking hard toward that shore." He pointed toward the northeast shore. "This wind is carrying us downstream too fast." He thought the increased exercise might help keep her warm. And they did need to get closer to that shore to keep from being carried around the end of the spit by the current.

Roy knew they would have to keep swimming if they were going to get to the spit before the current swept them around the end of it. If that happened, they would be in big trouble.

But he also knew they would have to pace themselves like long distance runners or swimmers. They may need a big kick finish. They would only get one chance.

They swam hard for about five minutes. And Roy said, " Now lets swim a little slower and get our breath." He checked their position. And it looked like they had made some progress.

He had been watching Linda closely and could see no change in her coordination. Her lips were still slightly blue but she seemed alert. And he couldn't tell if she was still shivering or not.

" Let's change ends of the cooler. I'll swim right-handed for a while and you swim left handed; that will rest us. If you start getting tired you must tell me, honey. I need to know how you are feeling."

Linda said, " I think it will feel good to switch ends for a while. We are gaining, aren't we, Roy?"

" Yes, we are making progress, but we better get busy. Let's hit it hard for a few more minutes then we'll check it again."

With that Roy started swimming. He was using long, strong strokes. He could tell Linda was not stroking as strong as she had when they started. He looked ahead; he could see they were gaining.

This stint ran longer than five minutes and when he looked again he was very much encouraged by their progress, but he was becoming more concerned about Linda. When he called a short rest, he hugged her and could feel her shivering more than before. He looked at his watch, it was a little after ten, and he estimated it would be another twenty-five minutes or more before they could wade ashore.

" How are we doing, Roy," Linda asked.

" We're doing fine, honey. About two more short spurts of hard swimming will put us close enough to shore that we will be able to make a landing somewhere along that spit. When we get close we will probably have to kick pretty hard to pull out of that current. But then we will only be a few yards from shore, and, I hope we can wade those last few yards."

Roy had been kicking and stroking with his one hand as he talked. He checked his bearings once again and saw that they were still gaining.

He said, "Do you want to switch again, Linda?"

"I think so," she said. "I was getting pretty tired this way."

As they were switching ends, Roy gave her another hug. She was still shivering; maybe not as much as before, but still shivering.

Roy knew he was getting tired and he was feeling the effect of the cold water but the wind wasn't so strong as they got closer to the shore. The sun had just been obscured by the clouds, but it peeped through intermittently, and as yet there was no rain.

When they had each gotten into position on either end of the cooler, Roy said,

O.K., honey, let's kick hard for another five minutes or so, and then take another reading."

Linda agreed and started to kick and stroke.

Roy's concern for Linda's well being was increasing. He realized she was not as animated and alert as she had been when they went into the water. He certainly had to admire her effort, but he could see she was tiring fast.

At this same time less than a half-mile away up the hill Herman and Tildy were getting ready to drive down to look at the water and take some pictures.

Herman said, "Tildy, where is that film we bought last Saturday? I can't take any pictures with an empty camera." He was rummaging through a kitchen drawer.

"Look in the overhead cabinet on the end," Tildy answered.

" Which end," Herman asked.

"The end over the refrigerator," she said from the bathroom."

He found the film just where she had said it would be.

He started to grab a pair of boots when he got to the porch, but Tildy said,

"Just forget the boots, Herman. If those sneakers get muddy I'll just wash them. We'll have to hurry a little or I won't have time to make lunch and I know you'll be hungry."

"We ought to take the binoculars too," he said." It's going to look a lot different than we've ever seen it."

"Oh, all right," she said. Then she hurried back into the house to get the binoculars.

Down in the water Roy and Linda had just finished another five or six minute push toward shore. When Roy checked their position, he happily told Linda they were in the chute and now the current would carry them toward their goal, until they had to pull out of the current just before reaching the spit.

Linda did not comment when Roy told her the good news.

Roy realized that she was still kicking and stroking but her coordination was off. While he was swimming, he hadn't noticed but now it was obvious that she was in trouble. He quickly moved around the cooler and took her in his arms. She was moving like an automaton. She did not respond to his embrace.

He said sharply, "Linda! Look at me."

She kept moving, but slowly tried to focus her eyes on Roy.

Roy hugged her body as close to his own as he could and gradually her attempts to swim subsided.

She looked at Roy with eyes filled with confusion. And when they finally focused on Roy, she put both arms around him and moaned softly, "Roy, I' I' I 'm'm c'c'cold."

Roy was as near panic as he had ever been in his life. They were going to be in the water at least ten more minutes. It would take at least that long to reach any shore and the spit they were aiming for was still their best bet.

Linda was going to need to be warmed up as soon as possible.

Roy knew from some of the recent first aid classes he had taken, at Hank's insistence, that she was entering a dangerous stage of hypothermia.

When he got her ashore he would have no way to build a fire, no blankets, no shelter but the poncho if it started to rain until he could get her to the old building.

He placed Linda's left hand through the handle of the cooler, then got behind her and held onto her hand and the same handle with his left hand. Then he started stroking with his right hand and kicking with his feet as hard as he could.

In two or three minutes Roy was very tired. He stopped swimming and just held Linda close, hoping his body heat would help a little.

The current was taking them directly toward the spot Roy hoped to wade ashore, but he knew the current had to turn sharply to the right sometime before they got to that desired spot. When the current made that turn, Roy knew he would have to swim hard to break free from the pull of that current.

He continued to hold Linda close. At this point she was lethargic and only mumbled softly, occasionally.

Roy was saving his strength for that last hard drive to the shore and the current was taking them ？ ？

Roy heard something! A motor? An engine? Roy knew engines? He knew it was a truck or an automobile running in a low gear. It was getting closer!

Roy thought he got a glimpse of chrome or something shining through the brush on the hillside, then it was gone, but he could still hear the engine getting closer.

There it was! Up there by the old building! A dark blue or gray pickup truck! It stopped!

Roy and Linda were still nearly fifty yards from the spit, and the truck had stopped up the hill at least one hundred yards from the water.

It was almost time for Roy to start to try to break away from the current.

Linda was conscious, but listless.

It was going to be difficult to pull out of the current. He would hold on to Linda and the cooler too. If he didn't land at the spit they would need the cooler to keep them afloat in the open water again.

Roy was watching the truck and people were getting out of it.

Roy shouted as loud as he could, *"**Help!---- Help!----- We Need Help!"***

Chapter 27

Enter Herman And Tildy

Herman let the pickup idle to a stop just a few yards downhill from the old barn.

Good Lord, Herman! Tildy exclaimed, "I had no idea there would be that much water!"

Herman said, "It's the most water that's been in this valley in my lifetime, even when it was still a swamp. It'll be a long, long time going down."

He shut off the engine and they opened the doors to get out, as Herman said, "There will be no crop in these bottoms this year."

Tildy stepped down from the cab, and said, "This is terr'----What was that! I heard some one yelling! Sounded like they said Help! There it is again! From out in the water, I think. That direction?" She pointed out toward the spit.

Herman hurried around the truck to look where she was pointing.

"There, Herman! I heard it again! Did you hear it?"

Herman started down the hill. "Yes, I heard it that time! Let's go!"

At age seventy-five and seventy-four they were neither one capable of actually running. But they hurried as fast as they dared.

There was a large cluster of blackberry briars between them and the water and when they got around them they could see the edge of the water.

Roy and Linda had reached the place where the current made its sharp bend to go around the peninsula and at this point it speeded up considerably.

Linda was in a state of semi consciousness. She was unable to help and Roy was almost completely exhausted. He was holding Linda's left hand to the handle of the cooler with his left hand and kicking and stroking with his right hand with all his might.

Twice more he gave a shout for help and then used the last of his energy to break free of the pull of the current. When he thought he was only going to be able to make a few more strokes, he felt a stick with his right hand and grabbed it like "Proverbial man, grasping at straws"

It held!

It was the top branch of a small sapling!

Roy gripped it tight and just hung there gasping for breath. He could see they were just on the edge of the current. Another half dozen good strong strokes and they would be in relatively still water. And with another few strokes after that he was sure he could wade the rest of the way.

The current was still tugging at them but Roy pulled them up closer and got a better grip on the sapling. He knew now that they could make it to land, but he was frantic with worry about Linda. He had been able to keep her face out of the water by holding to the cooler handle with her hand under his and her head on his shoulder and neck, but she was near losing consciousness completely. He had to get her warmed up immediately.

When Herman and Tildy got around the large briar patch, Herman said, "There he is! There's two of 'em! They're holding on to a big box of some kind!"

They were still a hundred yards from where Roy was floundering, making his last few strokes.

Roy shouted again, "***HELP!**"*

Herman could see the young man was all used up.

When Roy grabbed the sapling and stopped stroking, Herman thought they were going under.

By the time they got to the water's edge Roy had caught his breath and with one great pull on the sapling he started to swim those last few strokes.

He had less reserve left than he had thought and by the time he could put his feet down and wade, he took three steps and could go no farther. He just stood there in water up to his stomach desperately trying to move forward and holding on to Linda. His legs would not obey him.

"Please help us," he begged.

He swayed on his feet and almost went down.

"We need help."

By this time Herman was wading out to meet them.

Roy pleaded, "Can you help me build a fire? I've got to get Linda warm."

"Hypothermia!"

"Please help me get her warm."

Herman was in the water over his knees, and Roy with the last of his strength took three more steps and met him.

Herman grabbed Linda under the armpits, and walking backwards he dragged her out of the water.

Tildy then took Linda and eased her down to the ground while Herman went back to help Roy.

Roy wouldn't turn loose of the cooler, but with newfound strength in his legs he stumbled to the land and immediately jerked the cooler open. He grabbed the shirts and started to wrap Linda as best he could with the two garments.

Tildy was on her knees beside Linda, helping Roy.

"Please help me b b build a fire," Roy begged. "I've g g got to g g get her w w w warm."

Tildy said soothingly, "We'll get her in the truck. The heater will be warm, and when we get her to the house we'll get her into a tub of warm water."

For the first time Roy looked up into the kind face of the elderly lady that was helping him.

"Young man, you are not more than a few minutes from being in the same shape she's in. Your teeth are chattering, and your lips are blue. You are cold too," she said.

"In just a minute Herman will be down here with the truck and we'll get you both into the warm cab and to the house."

Tildy could see the tears of gratitude in Roy's eyes as he said, "Oh thank you M M Ma'am I'll p p pay you any thing you ask if you c c can help L L Linda."

Linda was incoherent, sometimes mumbling a few words, not moving much. Once she grabbed Roy and hugged him tightly and mumbled, "love you, Roy." She didn't open her eyes but just sagged back in Roy's arms.

Roy sat on the ground and held her as close as he could trying to keep the two shirts around her.

Now out of the water and with their wet clothes on, the light wind that was blowing made it seem several degrees colder than it really was.

Roy heard the pickup start, then the low grind of the gears in four-wheel drive coming down the hill.

Herman bounced down the hill and drove out onto the spit as far as he dared. He knew if he got too close to the water the ground would be too soft to support the truck. He stopped about twenty yards uphill from where they were.

Roy started to get up before the truck stopped. He tried to pick Linda up to carry her to the truck, but he was too weak.

Tildy said, "Let's try to walk her. It will be better for her if she will try to help." They stood her between them and started to walk slowly toward the pickup. Linda's legs moved jerkily but she was supporting herself partially and moving more or less automatically with a shuffling step at the urging of Roy and Tildy.

Tildy said, "This will help get some circulation going."

Herman had hopped out of the truck and hurried back and grabbed the cooler. He passed them and put the cooler in the back of the truck, and then he turned back and helped get Linda in the cab. The heat was blowing full blast.

Roy was shivering uncontrollably as he started to climb into the back of the truck. Herman firmly took his arm and said, "No, son, you get in the cab where it's warm. I'll ride in the back. Tildy will drive."

Roy looked at him with such gratitude that Herman felt a deep sense of compassion for this exhausted, desperate young stranger.

Roy did as he was told.

Chapter 28

Hypothermia! Linda Is Critical

Herman hurried around and opened the tailgate and climbed in the back and stood with his hands on top of the cab.

Tildy got into the driver's seat and put the truck in reverse. Using the outside rear view mirrors, she backed up until they were clear of the spit and there was enough space to turn the truck around. She expertly whipped it around and put it in a forward low gear and took it up the hill as fast as the rough terrain would allow.

As soon as they were going forward Tildy said,

"Roy, that is your name, I guess?"

Roy replied, "Yes, Ma'am."

Tildy continued, "How long have you been out there in the water?"

Roy looked at the dashboard clock. It read 10:45.

"I g g guess about an hour and a half, this t time."

"Where did you start from?" she asked.

"That big sycamore tree," he said.

Tildy looked at him sharply. She thought, "I wonder if he knows what he's saying."

Linda stirred and mumbled something Roy could not understand. He said, "It's all right honey, we are going to get warm now. I think these folks saved our lives."

Tildy thought, "He sounds all right now, but I won't ask any more questions right now."

Roy said, "We're awfully dirty, Ma'am. I'm afraid we're really messing up your nice pickup. We haven't had a bath or clean clothes since Saturday morning."

He was starting to warm up, his teeth had stopped chattering, but he still felt really cold.

They could see the house now, on up the hill another three hundred yards or so.

Tildy said, "When we get to the house we'll rush Linda in, and we'll run the water and get her in it, maybe clothes and all, and I'll fix you both some hot tea."

"That will really be wonderful, Ma'am. We haven't had anything to drink, except Pepsi Cola, since Saturday morning. I think we are probably a little dehydrated too."

Tildy didn't know what to think about the things Roy was saying but she knew Linda was in dire need of help and that Roy was almost as bad off as Linda. And she also knew that she and Herman would not deny them that help.

She would worry about the strange story later.

Roy admired the familiar way she handled the pickup. She was a small woman, still a pretty woman, Roy thought, probably fifty-five or sixty years old. And since she was a farm wife, Roy figured she could handle a tractor or a semi with the same confidence as she did the pickup.

She wheeled into the driveway and stopped near the back door with the passenger side next to the house. She quickly got out and came around to help Roy get Linda out. Herman went ahead and held the door open so they could walk Linda in.

Linda seemed a little steadier on her feet than before.

Tildy said, "Right through here," and led Linda and Roy through the kitchen into a short hallway and then left into a spacious bathroom. It was spotless and decorated in various shades of blue.

She let Roy hold Linda while she turned on the water and adjusted the temperature. While the water was running, she left the room and returned in just a few seconds with two bathrobes, obviously one for each of them. She hung them both on the same hook behind the door.

"Now," she said. "lets get her out of these dirty clothes and into the warm water."

Roy stammered, "Ma'am, we are not married yet. But we are going to be just as soon as we can."

Tildy looked up at Roy in surprise. "You're Not?"

With the slightest delay, Tildy said,

"Well, do you love her?"

Roy soberly said, "I sure do, Ma'am."

"Well, then help me get these cold, wet, dirty clothes off of her and get her into this warm water. And then if you want to you can wait in the kitchen while I give her a good bath."

Roy held her up while Tildy took Linda's blouse and bra off. Then Tildy undid Linda's jeans and slid them down and her panties came down at the same time.

"Now, hold her up while I lift her feet out of her pants."

Roy put his arms around her waist and lifted her up while Tildy pulled the soggy garments off of her feet.

She was completely naked, but Roy was so concerned about her condition that he hardly noticed.

She could support at least part of her own weight, but without Roy to help she would have collapsed.

Tildy lifted her feet into the tub one at a time, and Roy eased her down into the warm water.

Linda was slowly becoming more alert but Roy was getting colder still in his wet clothes.

Tildy noticed Roy's discomfort, and said, "You are starting to chill again, aren't you?"

Roy nodded and said, "Yes, M, M, Ma'am," his teeth were chattering again.

Tildy said, "You stay here with Linda for just a minute, I'll be right back." And then she hurried out.

She returned in less than a minute with a pair of insulated coveralls, which she handed to Roy.

"Take these into the bedroom across the hall and get out of those wet clothes and put these on. When we get Linda warmed up, you will get in the tub," she ordered. Then she turned back to Linda, whose eyes were starting to focus as she looked around the strange room.

Roy stepped out of the bathroom and across the hall into the bedroom. He noticed immediately the faint odor of perfume, or powder, definitely a girl's room, a bright, cheerful room with a light green carpeted floor, a beautifully decorated bedroom suite, a large walk in closet well stocked with feminine clothing, and there were pastel green curtains at the window.

Roy quickly peeled off the wet tee shirt and his pants and jockey shorts. He was shivering and his teeth were chattering. He pulled on the heavy coveralls and just got them zipped up, when he heard Linda crying from the bathroom. "Roy! Roy! Where are you? Roy!"

In two steps he was across the hall and in the bathroom. Linda was struggling, trying to get up and out of the bathtub. Roy dropped to his knees beside the bathtub and took both her hands in his. As soon as she saw his face she stopped struggling.

She said, "Roy, where were you? Where are we?"

"Linda, honey, we are safe now; we are going to be O.K.," Roy explained, " We are in Herman and Tildy's house. We are out of the tree and we're getting baths and getting warm, and everything is going to be O.K. now."

"And now," Tildy said, "I'm going to get that hot tea and we'll all have a cup. I'll be right back."

When the door closed Linda put one hand behind Roy's head and pulled him to her for a kiss.

"Roy, what happened? We were kicking and swimming and I was getting pretty cold and we were a long way from our tree, and then I don't remember."

Roy gently answered, "I'm sorry, honey. It was too cold this morning and we were too weak. You were overcome by hypothermia, but I didn't know how fast it could wear us down. Another ten minutes in the water and we wouldn't have made it. I knew it would be tough, but the wind was against us and that made it tougher and that also made us colder."

"If it wasn't for Herman and Tildy, we would have either floated around the spit and back out to open water, or I would still be down there in the brush, trying to start a fire by rubbing two wet sticks together. We almost didn't make it, honey."

Tildy knocked on the door. Roy looked surprised, and said, "Come in," and then got up to open the door.

Tildy came in with a large tray with a teapot, three cups already filled, some napkins, and a plate of sugar cookies. "We'll just have a short tea party now," she said, "and we'll have lunch a little later, if we can get you two warmed up. Herman is having his tea and cookies at the kitchen table but he won't want to miss lunch. We're having chicken soup for lunch."

She set the tray on the sink counter top and gave the first cup to Linda--sat it on the edge of the tub. Roy sat on the only chair with his cup, and she sat on the stool after she had passed the cookies around, urging them to take a handful.

Tildy knew the hot tea would help to warm them, and she wanted to see how fast the cookies disappeared. They had neither one said anything about being hungry, and she hadn't asked, but she knew they probably were very hungry. She loved to cook and was already planning meals for tomorrow.

She watched them eat, pleased that the cookies were almost gone. She filled their teacups again, and said, "Linda, are you feeling better now?"

Linda said, "Yes, Tildy? I want to thank you from the bottom of my heart. You don't even know us, and you couldn't have been nicer. I've heard you mention Herman? And I want to thank him too."

Roy said, "Herman pulled you ashore, when I couldn't go any farther."

Tildy said, "Roy, are you getting warmer?"

"Yes, Ma'am, these coveralls are really helping a lot."

"O.K. Linda, if you feel like you would be steady enough on your feet and want to, you can stand up, drain this dirty water, and pull the shower curtain and take a shower and wash your hair. There is shampoo on the shelf. And when you are finished Roy can have the bathroom. I'm going out to fix our chicken soup. And I'll throw these dirty clothes in the washer. You two are on your own. It'll be ready in about forty five minutes." She picked up the tray and the cups and Linda's dirty clothes and left.

Linda slowly got to her feet, with Roy's help. She felt very unsteady, even with Roy's arms around her. After a few seconds she tried standing without Roy supporting her. It was then she realized she was naked.

"Oh, Roy, I'm so embarrassed. I'm acting completely shameless." She pulled the shower curtain around to cover her self. "I guess I've not been thinking too well. Was I talking silly?"

Roy said, " No, Honey, you hardly talked at all and you didn't say anything wrong. You were so cold that you almost lost consciousness. You had me very worried. How do you feel now?"

"I think I'll be all right now. I think it will feel good to wash my hair. Please stay in here with me while I do it, in case I get real weak. I may need help."

"O.K, honey, I'll be right here," Roy promised, as she pulled the curtain the rest of the way around and opened the drain.

When the shower started running, Roy sat on the chair. He was more exhausted than he thought. He was warming up nicely in the insulated coveralls but he was very tired. He was thinking about Herman and Tildy. What would he have done without their help? Linda had reached the point where, without heat, she would have been critical in just a short time. He would not have been able to continue much longer himself.

Linda said, "Do you see any towels, Roy?"

"I'll look," he said. "There's a cabinet here by the door. I'll look there."

He opened the door to disclose a large stack of towels, washcloths, soap, shampoo, toothpaste, sunscreen, toilet paper, everything you would find in a bathroom closet,

"Yeah, here are the towels," he said. He took a towel from the stack and stood by the curtain, as she turned the water off.

" O.K. I'm ready," she said, and stuck a hand over the curtain to receive the towel.

Roy handed her the towel and took the smallest bathrobe down from the hook and held it ready for her.

When she was through drying, she wrapped the towel around herself and stepped out of the tub and stumbled against Roy. He caught her in his arms, and they both almost went down.

"We are both much weaker than we think we are," Roy said. " It will take a day or two to recover from this ordeal."

"I know, Roy. Thinking about it all, while I was in the shower, it scares me, and I'm so grateful to Tildy and Herman. We don't even know their last name." She turned around and slipped her arms into the bathrobe and released the towel and said,

"You had better get in the shower; we certainly don't want to be late for lunch. And as tired you are, I know it will make you feel better. I think I should go out now and give Tildy a progress report, but I'll be back to hand you the towel when you're ready."

Roy said, "As soon as I get clean I want a kiss."

She started toward him. He put his hands out to hold her back. "Not 'till I get clean. You are so clean and pretty now. I'll hurry because I desperately want that kiss."

Linda said, "I don't really want to wait, but I will if you insist."

As soon as she went out of the door, Roy took the coveralls off and hurried into the shower. It was the most appreciated shower he had ever taken.

Chapter 29

At Herman and Tildy's House

Linda left the bathroom and turned toward the sounds and smells that she assumed were coming from the kitchen. She did not remember being led through the house to the bathroom. She vaguely remembered Herman helping her out of the water. And the next thing she could remember was Roy easing her down into the wonderful, warm water.

She was very weak and unsteady, and Tildy, looking alarmed met her in the hall.

"Linda, do you feel like walking? Here, sit here." She pulled a chair away from the table and took Linda's arm and helped her sit down.

After the shower and walking those few steps, Linda was ready to rest and was grateful for the chair.

"I'm sorry," she said. "I guess I'm not as strong as I thought I was."

Tildy said, "I think you are doing very well. I wasn't sure you could take a shower by yourself. But I knew Roy would help, if you needed help."

Herman was sitting at the table and had been looking at the newspaper and alternately listening to the conversation.

Linda looked at him and at Tildy and said, "We are so very grateful to you both. We can, and we will, pay you for the kindness you are showing."

"Nonsense!" Herman said. "We won't be paid for just doing the right thing, and I don't want to hear anymore about it. Is Roy O.K.?"

Linda said, "I think he is O.K. but very tired. We really haven't had much real rest since last Friday night. I think I'd better go back in the bathroom and hand him a towel when he is finished with his shower."

Tildy walked back to the bathroom door with Linda, gently touching her elbow. Linda was pretty wobbly.

Tildy said, "Lunch will be ready in about ten or fifteen minutes. Just come to the kitchen in the bathrobes, and after we eat, we'll see about finding something for you both to wear. Do you feel warm now, Linda?"

"Yes, I think I'm doing O.K. now, but I'm so weak and shaky."

"Some of this chicken soup and a good rest will help that, I'm sure."

Linda's hand was on the doorknob, and Tildy said, "Come on out to the kitchen when Roy is ready." And she hurried back down the short hallway.

Linda went in and when Roy heard the door open he said, "You are right on time." He turned the water off and said, " I'm ready for the towel."

Linda took another towel from the stack and handed it over the curtain, and said, "Tildy says lunch will be ready in about ten minutes. It really smells good."

Roy took the towel and said, "I'll really miss the peanut butter crackers and the warm Pepsi. Won't you?"

Linda laughed and said, "Roy Johnson, you have a twisted mind."

Roy finished drying and wrapped the towel around himself, pulled back the shower curtain, and stepped out.

Linda met him before he got both feet on the floor. "I'm ready for that clean kiss and I don't want to wait until you shave."

He took her in his arms, drew her close, and kissed her passionately.

Suddenly, he released her and jerked his arms down and grabbed the towel. "The knot came undone." He grinned, as he refastened the towel.

"Help me into that other bathrobe and we'll start over."

"Oh, Roy, I love your sense of humor," she said as she held the bathrobe for him.

He tied the robe in front and let the towel drop, then turned around and kissed her again without interruption.

When they stopped to breathe Linda said, "We should go to the kitchen. "

Roy said, "Like this! In a bathrobe?"

Tildy said to eat in the bathrobes, and after lunch, she will find something for us to wear."

They went down the hall to the kitchen, hand in hand.

Roy felt weak and trembley. He knew he had pushed himself to the limit when Herman grabbed Linda and dragged her to shore. And he knew now that by the time he would have recovered enough to carry Linda and wade out of the water by himself, he would have collapsed. There would not have been much he could have done to get her warm. He shuddered to think what might have happened if Herman and Tildy had not been there.

He suddenly felt very self-conscious in the home of these kind strangers, dressed only in a bathrobe. It wasn't even his bathrobe.

They entered the kitchen as Tildy set the large bowl of hot, steaming, chicken soup in the middle of the table.

Herman was just entering the kitchen from another room. He walked straight to Roy and stuck out his hand.

"Are you feeling better now, Roy? I think you were just about all used up by the time you got into the pickup."

" Yes sir," Roy said, shaking Herman's hand. "I was awfully cold, and so tired I could hardly walk. I don't know what we would have done if you folks hadn't been there. I want to thank you a whole lot, and, Sir, we don't even know your name."

"Well, son, I'm Herman Schultze and that's Tildy, short for Matilda."

"I want to pay you for all your kindness and your hospitality," Roy said, and Linda was nodding affirmatively.

Herman was moving his head side to side.

"We don't take pay for hospitality in these parts."

"We are both just glad we were able to help you. And now let's set down and have some of that soup."

The table was set for four, with a delicious looking small, garden salad at each place. There were three different types of salad dressing on the table, a loaf of homemade bread, a pitcher of iced tea, a pitcher of water, and a large glass filled with ice at each place.

Tildy said, "That's Herman's place there on the end. You two sit any place you want, and I'll take what's left. Do you want water or tea to drink?"

Linda said, "I'd like water please. We haven't had water to drink since last Friday."

Roy said, "Me too, please. Water sure sounds good."

Tildy filled their glasses and set the pitcher on their corner of the table.

When Tildy had sat down, Linda and Roy both picked up their water glass and drank deeply. Roy drained his and there wasn't much left in Linda's glass when she set it down.

"My Goodness. You kids were really thirsty. You really haven't had a drink of water since last Friday?"

"We want to hear the whole story but let's eat first," Tildy said. " It's no wonder you're weak; let's get some food in you. Roy, take that pitcher and fill those water glasses again and then dip up some soup or start on you're salad whichever you want first."

Herman said, "Let's start with soup, Roy, I think you both need some of that hot chicken soup right now. And here, take a slice of Tildy's home made bread. It's special."

Roy and Linda ate with enthusiasm. Herman and Tildy kept urging them to eat more, have another slice of bread, have another bowl of soup, more tea? etc.

Finally Roy said, "We probably shouldn't eat so much since this is our first real meal since Saturday morning. It is delicious." Linda broke in agreeing with Roy wholeheartedly.

"It really is delicious and Roy is right, we'd better stop before we make ourselves sick. We couldn't have had a better meal for our first meal. Chicken soup is the best thing we could have had for the shape we were in and could I please have the recipe?"

Tildy blushed with pride, and Herman said,

"Everybody wants Tildy's recipe for chicken soup."

Tildy said, "You will be very welcome to the recipe but it's mostly just a pinch of this and a dab of that. It's in my recipe book. You can copy it tomorrow. But now, if you two feel up to it, we would like to hear how you happened to be in the water so far from any road."

Roy spoke, "I don't hardly know where to start but I guess last Thursday would be a good beginning."

Linda nodded agreeably and smiled. They were holding hands. "That was before we knew each other," she said.

Herman and Tildy's eyebrows went up simultaneously.

Roy said, "I guess there will be lots of surprises in this story. It would take three days to tell all that happened. So, I'll just hit the high spots. The most important thing is, Linda and I met, and from now on we will always be together." Again Linda smiled and nodded.

They took turns telling the story.

It was late afternoon when Linda and Roy reached the point in their story where Roy heard Herman's pickup arriving at the old barn.

Outside, the rain that had started in the early afternoon still drummed heavily on the roof.

Chapter 30

Monday Afternoon Sam's Office

Monday at 1:00 P.M. Sam, Dusty, Wilford, and all four State Troopers met in Sam's office.

Matthew was talking to headquarters on Sam's phone.

"Yes sir, we will go back down and do a thorough search of the surrounding area------- Yes sir, tomorrow morning ------- Yes sir, I will request that the men that found the vehicles will be there also----Yes sir, thank you, sir."

He hung up the phone and said to the group, "The Captain wants us to search the vehicles for obvious mechanical problems and to search the area around the vehicles for anything that may have contributed to an accident."

"He is sending an accident reconstruction expert who will need a detailed report on everything, from the initial discovery of the vehicles, the road conditions before the road was flooded, the dives, everything. He will ask a lot of questions."

Sam asked, "What time in the morning will this all start?"

"At ten o-clock," Matthew replied. "We'll all meet at the water's edge on road eleven at ten."

As planned, just before ten A.M. Tuesday morning, Wilford and Dusty launched their boat and pulled their trailer up out of the way, so the dive team members would have room to back down the road and launch their boat.

The rain that had started in the early morning had now stopped and the mist and fog that hung low over the water was lifting and would soon be dissipated.

Promptly at ten- o-clock the State Police pickup backed down the hill to unload their boat. Again the patrol car drove down almost to the water's edge. This time, Matthew was accompanied by two men. Sarge and the other officer in uniform was Captain Dillon the accident reconstruction expert.

Bob and George had their craft in the water in a matter of minutes and pulled up alongside their trailer.

Wilford and Dusty pulled up on the other side of the trailer.

Matthew introduced Capt. Dillon to Will and Dusty and asked if the Captain could ride in their boat. This would put three men in each boat and give the Captain opportunity to question Wilford and Dusty about the road conditions and how the land laid beneath the water.

Matthew would again pilot the dive team boat and Sarge would stay in the patrol car, as before, to relay information to headquarters.

Dusty was at the controls and Capt. Dillon said, "Is everybody ready to go?"

Matthew said, "We're ready, Sir."

Dusty said, "Yes, Sir"

"O.K. Let's go," the Captain, said.

Dusty revved up the engine and turned the boat around and proceeded down road eleven with the police boat in their wake.

The noise of the motor kept them from having a conversation, so for the next five minutes or so they rode in silence.

When they reached the Cyprus trees, Dusty cut the engine and turned on the trolling motor and Matthew did the same.

Matthew knew where to position the boat for the first dive, and Dusty moved in to a spot a few feet away.

Captain Dillon said, "O.K., guys, do a real close search all around this first vehicle. Look for any damage that may indicate contact with another vehicle or for that matter, any solid object.

Look for any thing that may have been knocked loose or could have fallen off of or out of the vehicle. Anything that's loose down there should be noted and recorded."

They both had their diving gear on and George went down first this time.

Capt. Dillon had a notepad and pencil ready. He asked Wilford and Dusty, "What does this countryside look like when it's not under water?"

They both started to answer. Dusty's answer came out first. "It is just a big, flat, level, valley bottom on both sides of the road. Those three Cyprus trees," he said gesturing toward the trees, "are about the only thing that grows here for a mile or more in any direction, except corn."

Wilford said, "Those trees were planted when the culvert under the road was installed eight or nine years ago. The culvert is just about twelve feet east of that first tree. I'm sure because I helped install it and I also helped plant the trees."

"Do you think the culvert could have in any way contributed to an accident?" asked the Captain.

"No way," said Wilford. " I drove this road Friday evening, and the culvert was under water on both ends. You wouldn't have even known it was there."

"O.K., guys. I just want to check every possibility." He was making notes of everything that was said.

The rain started again, no thunder and lightning, just a steady drenching rain

George had been down almost five minutes. He came up beside the boat and said, " I found one interesting thing. One cowboy boot, a left boot, size eleven. It was about thirty five or forty feet from either vehicle, over in that direction." He pointed more or less toward the south. I left it in that same spot. I only moved it enough to read the label. It's a Tony Lama, and it looks to be in good shape."

"Any thing else, George?" Capt. Dillon asked.

George answered, "Yes, sir, right beside the pickup bed there is a padlocked tool box, about thirty inches long, twelve or fourteen inches wide and about that deep. It's lying on its side with the padlocked lid toward the truck bed. It looks like a nice one. The rest of it is just like Bob said; the left door is the only visible damage. We can range out further and maybe find another boot. The water is a little clearer today than it was yesterday."

"O.K., George, that gives me a pretty good picture. Let's see what the other vehicle yields."

Matthew maneuvered the boat into position and Bob made this dive. He was back up in less than three minutes.

"The Escort has a broken fan belt!" he said, as soon as he could spit out the mouthpiece." I just made one circle around the car and then I examined under the hood. So far that's all I found."

"That broken fan belt is significant," The Captain said.

Bob said, " I'll go back down now and search a wider area." and he was gone again.

The Captain was making notes and estimating the distance from the vehicles to the Cyprus trees and from one vehicle to the other. He asked, "Does this road run due east and west?"

"Yes sir," Wilford said, "by the compass. It was first laid out by the Army Corp of Engineers and the State and the County followed their orders."

"Then it looks like that levee that broke runs a pretty true north and south."

"That's right," Wilford said. "Nobody thought it would ever break, but nobody remembers ever getting this much rain. It's sure been awful and now these two vehicles,"--- He paused for a moment----and then, "I just hope there wasn't any little kids in either one of them."

The Captain listened to Wilford without speaking and then resumed his notes. He turned up a new sheet on his notepad, holding it under a piece of clear plastic to shelter it from the rain and started drawing a map.

Dusty watched closely. It was plain to see he was drawing the underwater road, the Cyprus trees, and the position of the car and pickup that lay on the bottom.

Dusty thought he's really good. If you actually measured it out, it would be very near a scale drawing.

Bob surfaced beside Wilford's boat this time. Holding on to the side of the boat with one hand he removed his mouthpiece. He said, "I didn't find anything new. I found the boot that George found and nothing else but a muddy bottom."

"O.K., boys," the Captain said, looking out from under his rain hood. "We'll take this information back to headquarters, and I'll get with a couple more reconstruction people, and we'll try to have a composite situation, or maybe two or three possible, hypothetical, situations to think about. There are no witnesses, so it will actually be hypothetical. We should have some information concerning the license plate numbers by tomorrow afternoon, but for now that's about all we can do. So let's load up and go to lunch."

Chapter 31

Linda Starting to Recover

Tildy said, "This has really been a good story. You kids should write a book."

"I'm glad you were able to--live--in that tree," Herman said slowly. "And I'm glad we decided to drive down to look at the water this morning."

"Me too," Roy said. "I think now, looking back, I would probably have passed out if we had made it to land. And in that wind and being wet and the condition I was in-----we owe you folks for our lives."

"Well," Tildy said, "I told you we would find something for you both to wear. Come with me."

She led the way into the room where Roy had stripped off his wet clothes and put on the coveralls.

She said, "This was our son Willie's room originally, but he was grown, married, and on his own by the time our daughter Francine came along. Twenty-one years between them. So then, this was Francine's room."

"Francine is an E.R. nurse at the big hospital up in Peoria. She comes home for a weekend about once a month. She'll probably get to come home on the week end of the Fourth of July."

"She has lots of clothes, shoes, underclothes, everything, Linda, and she is about your size, choose anything you like. I'm sure she won't mind."

She was interrupted by the telephone. "I'll have to get that. Herman has gone outside to get your cooler out of the truck and put the truck in the garage."

The phone rang again as she was talking.

She picked up the phone that sat on the small desk. " Hello, Tildy here"-------.

"Francine! I didn't expect to hear from you before Friday,"

Roy and Linda watched her turn pale as she listened.

"Are you hurt? Are you all right?"

Another short pause. She gripped the phone tighter.

"Oh, Francine, honey, did you have surgery? ------Were you admitted? ------A moon boot ----crutches?"

Another pause, longer this time.

Herman came into the room and said, "I thought I heard the phone ring." Then he saw the look on Tildy's face.

"What happened?" he demanded! He looked at Tildy, then Roy, then Linda.

Roy said, "We don't know."

Linda put her hand on Herman's arm. "We think she's talking to your daughter Francine, and maybe she has had an accident."

Tildy was saying, "Yes, honey, you come straight home ------- Yes. Daddy will meet you at the Walmart Parking lot----Yes, we will meet you before ten o-clock."

She listened intently a little longer, holding her hand out as if to hold Herman back.

"Yes, I understand, honey. We'll be waiting when you get there----- Bye."

She went directly to Herman. "Francine has a broken leg," she said with trembling lips. "She is all right. Her car was hit broadside by a taxicab yesterday morning at six thirty on her way to work. The large bone in her lower left leg, it's not broken completely in two. She'll have to wear something called a moon boot for about three weeks, and she'll be on crutches for a while. She sounds O.K."

She turned toward Roy and Linda and said, "The doctors and the nurses, all, are her friends," and then she looked back at Herman. "They made her stay in the hospital last night. She said she would not have had to stay, but it was paid for and the cab company will repair or replace her car."

Herman had not said a word. He was letting Tildy tell the story in her own way.

Tildy continued, "They're leaving right away. Ryan wanted to bring her home but Francine insisted he stay. He has two really tough tests coming Friday."

"Esther is going to drive her home. You remember Esther? We met her Easter weekend when we drove up to see Francine?"

Tildy turned to Linda and Roy and explained, "Ryan is her fiancée."

Then back to Herman, "Francine wants us to meet her at Walmart parking lot so Esther won't have to drive the unfamiliar country roads back to the interstate, alone, after dark. She has to work tomorrow so she will have to return immediately. It's a little after four now so they should be in town by nine thirty."

Then Tildy looked stricken, and said, "My Goodness! Francine will need her room!"

"Linda, I meant for you and Roy to have this room. Or Roy could have the couch in the living room. Oh my. What will we do? Herman, what can we do?"

Before Herman could answer, Roy spoke, "Is there a motel in town? I don't even know what town we are near, but if there is a motel? ----When you go in to town to meet your daughter---if you could drop us off there we would be very grateful."

Herman said, "But we wanted you to stay here tonight, to visit some more."

Roy said, "We need to get to a store or some place where we can buy some clothes. A Walmart store should have everything we need to start with. And I would need to find a bank. I'll call my bank back home to wire us some money. We'll need a car or pickup or some kind of transportation."

Tildy said, "Oh, I'm so sorry. This isn't working out the way I wanted it to. Oh, yes, Roy, I washed your clothes. The things that were in your pockets are on top of the drier. I tried to separate things so they could dry. I'm afraid some of your pictures may be ruined. The money and your driver's license and credit cards are O.K. I'm sure. The small pocketknife and the odd change it's all there. The underwear and the tee shirt will probably never be white again as well as Linda's blouse and brassiere and under panties. Both pairs of jeans will be presentable. The two flannel shirts came out good."

Tildy said, "And, yes, there is a new Best Western motel in town about a block and a half down and across the street from Walmart. But I do hope you'll come back tomorrow noon. I'm planning to have a big fried chicken dinner with all the fixin's."

Linda said, "Oh, Tildy, you folks are so nice to us. We can't help but feel like we are imposing. You've already done so much for us."

"Just promise you will come tomorrow noon. We want you to meet Francine too," Tildy said.

"Let's go get your jeans out of the dryer; your other things have already been dried."

When they reached the utility room Roy saw the contents of his wallet spread out over the top of the dryer. Roy said, "I'll pick this stuff up a little later. It needs to dry a little more."

When Tildy handed Linda her jeans, Linda said, "I have a change of clothes in my Emergency Kit in the cooler."

"It's on the porch," Herman said.

Roy went with Herman to get Linda's small bag out of the cooler. He said, "If I can find the number and use your phone I'll see if I can get reservations for tonight at the motel. And If I can get the money wired and buy a vehicle, we can drive back out tomorrow for that big chicken dinner Tildy is planning. It sounds great."

Herman said, "Tildy don't do anything halfway. It will be good."

When they got back, Linda and Tildy were in Francine's room again. Tildy had Roy's neatly folded jeans, under wear and tee shirt in a small stack on the bed. The flannel shirts were on hangers.

Roy handed the small bag to Linda, and Tildy said,

"You can get dressed here if you like, Linda, and help yourself to any of Francine's things you may need. She has another complete wardrobe in her apartment. And, Roy, Herman will show you to our room, where you can do the same. Shoes may be the only problem."

Roy picked up his freshly laundered clothes and followed Herman down the hallway to the next bedroom.

Herman said, "This is our room and that's my closet over there." He motioned to the left.

It was a large room with the head of a king size bed against the far wall, a window on each side of the bed, and a huge walk in closet on the right, obviously, Tildy's side of the room. A dresser and chest of drawers on the right side of the door revealed Tildy's taste in cosmetics and beauty care. On the left a door opened into the master bathroom. It was even larger than the bathroom where Linda and Roy had showered. The rest of the left wall was another large walk in closet. Through the open closet door Roy could see Herman's clothes, nicer dress clothes on one side and work clothes on the other. Several pairs of shoes lined the back wall of the closet floor.

"Just use anything you need here, Roy. I'll look up the number of the motel while you're getting dressed. I hope you will be able to wear a pair of those shoes," Herman said, as he walked down the hall.

Roy closed the door and took off the borrowed bathrobe and put on his own clothes. The tee shirt was not as white as it had been, but as far as Roy was concerned it was clean and quite acceptable. He put the flannel shirt on over the tee shirt but did not tuck it in and left it unbuttoned. He found a pair of socks on a shelf in the closet and he took a pair of older looking sneakers from the row of shoes on the floor. The sneakers were a little tight, but he laced them loosely and they were going to be all right.

Herman met Roy in the hall with a slip of paper with the motel number on it. Roy said, "I'll have to get one of my credit cards before I call the motel. They'll want a number."

Herman said, "Use any phone you want."

Roy went to the utility room and picked up his credit card and saw Linda and Tildy through the open door of Francine's room. Knowing there was a phone in that room, he went in.

He said, "If I'm not interrupting anything, I'll call the motel from here."

Tildy said, "Linda is still not feeling well."

Roy hurried to Linda's side. She was sitting on the only chair in the room looking pale. He got down on one knee and took her hands in his. "Do you have fever? Do you feel sick?" he asked.

"No," Linda replied slowly. "I think I am just totally exhausted. I'm too tired to comb my hair."

Roy said, "Your hair looks beautiful just as it is. You just sit there and I'll put these shoes and socks on you while you rest."

He still had the credit card and the phone number in his hand. He said, "I'd better make the reservation first, and then we'll put these shoes on. You just relax."

He quickly picked up the phone and punched in the numbers. "Yes, Ma'am, my name is Roy Johnson. I'd like to reserve two adjoining rooms for tonight," a slight pause, and he recited his credit card number. "Yes, Ma'am, we should arrive between nine and ten---- yes, two people. Thank you."

He noticed a look of mild surprise on Tildy's face and a bewildered, sad look on Linda's face as he hung up the phone.

Tildy said, "It's almost six, I'll go fix supper." When she left the room she noticed the crestfallen look on Linda's face.

As soon as she was out of the room, Linda asked quietly, "Roy, why did you reserve two rooms?"

"So we would each have a private bath. You know, in all our time together, you've always had a private bathroom. All three days. And we don't want to give anyone, anything to gossip about," he said with an impish grin. He gathered her up in his arms and kissed her tenderly. "I don't think you'll ever be able to keep me out of your room whereever we stay."

Linda hugged him tightly with her lips against his neck, and said, "I don't ever want to sleep without you Roy. I want to be close to you, and I don't care what the gossips say or think."

She sat down and Roy put the socks and shoes on her feet. She was very weak.

Chapter 32

The Motel

Tildy had a puzzled frown on her face when she walked out of Francine's room. When it had been assumed that Roy and Linda would spend the night, Tildy had felt sure that they would have, by choice, shared the same room. She knew they weren't married and that didn't make any difference. They were both adults and Tildy knew they cared for each other. It just didn't sound right when Roy reserved two rooms after all they had been through together. She had heard Linda call out for Roy when she was hardly conscious, and she had seen Roy rush to her and had seen the concern in his expression. And, yes! love, in his touch.

Tildy turned these thoughts every which way in her mind as she prepared the simple meal, salad and sandwiches, with ice cream and angel food cake for dessert.

By the time everything was finished she had concluded, "I am not wrong about those two. One way or another they will be together for a long time."

She went to the door to tell Herman to come in as Linda and Roy walked in from the hall.

Linda looked very pretty in her pink sweater and beige pants. She was pale and very wobbly and unsteady on her feet, but Roy stayed close and kept a protective hand on her arm or on her back as he guided her carefully to a chair.

Tildy watched approvingly as Roy got her seated at the end of the table and patted her softly on the shoulder.

Herman pulled his chair out and said, "Let's sit, Roy. We'll have some supper before we go to town. If you want, we can go early and I'll show you where to find the banks and the auto dealers, and I think the Walmart store stays open 'till nine through the week, if you want to stop there before you go to the motel. Just so we can be at the Walmart parking lot before nine thirty."

It was a few minutes after six when they finished eating, and Tildy said, "I'll leave the dishes 'til morning. I'll just clear the table and change my top, and I'll be ready to go."

Linda tried to help, but Tildy said, "Linda you need rest more than I need help." She led Linda into the living room to a large recliner. She said, "You sit here while I get ready."

Linda gratefully sat down and leaned back and Tildy levered the handle so that Linda was practically lying down.

Tildy left the room and went to the kitchen to clear the table and put things in their place. She quickly finished that task and left Herman and Roy sitting at the table discussing how Roy could buy a pickup or a van and get it licensed and insured in time to drive out to Herman and Tildy's house for dinner tomorrow (Dinner, being the noon meal in farm country).

It was decided that Herman would drive into town at eight-o-clock in the morning to escort Roy and Linda around to the various auto dealers and eventually the license branch office and Roy's choice of insurance companies.

In a few minutes Tildy returned and announced she was ready.

Roy went with her to get Linda. When they entered the room it was obvious that Linda was asleep. Her face was turned toward the window, her right arm was relaxed at her side, and her left forearm lay limply across her stomach.

She stirred when she heard Tildy quietly say, "I think she is completely exhausted and I think you are too, Roy. We need to get you two settled in at the motel, soon."

"I agree", Roy replied.

Linda opened her eyes and smiled as Roy took hold of her hand.

"Is it time to go?" she asked, struggling to get out of the big recliner.

"Yes, and tonight we won't be sleeping under the poncho. We'll be warm and dry," Roy said, and he levered her back into a sitting position and helped her to her feet. He carried her Emergency Kit and kept a protective arm around her, as Tildy herded them through the kitchen and onto the back porch where Herman was waiting.

Herman had pulled their two-year-old Sedan Deville up to the same place that Tildy had stopped the pickup when they had arrived that morning.

Linda and Tildy rode in the back seat. Roy rode in the front with Herman so he could remember the twists and turns and crossroads on the winding, hilly blacktop on the twenty-five minute drive into town.

Hardinville had been a typical little Midwestern town, with the town square, a drugstore, a small movie theater, and two grocery stores, about a half-mile apart, two churches, and three gas stations. The county courthouse, of course, stood in the middle of the square, surrounded by several other small businesses, including the feed store, a hardware store, a barbershop, and Don and Belle's Family Tavern and Restaurant.

The population literally exploded when the new four-lane highway swept through the edge of town just six blocks from the courthouse. And then two manufacturing plants sprang up, one on either side of the highway, a half-mile south of town. The Walmart store and three automobile dealerships followed close on the heels of the two big manufacturing plants.

Herman drove into town on the street that passed the courthouse on the south side. He explained, "This street goes straight through town to the four lane and the north entrance / exit. It's not a cloverleaf, and neither is the south exit; this town is too small. Most of the traffic is down at the south exit by the two factories, and you can see the Walmart sign for a long way from either direction. And the Best Western sign is at that intersection too."

One block past the courthouse he stopped at a stop light, and since there was no traffic behind him, he sat there and pointed across the street; on the left was one of the two banks and the G. M. dealership that handled Chevrolet, Buick, Cadillac and G.M.C. pickups. They sported a large sign touting the skill of Mr. Goodwrench and their complete modern service department.

As he turned right onto the cross street, he was saying, "This is the main drag now, called Second Street. It is where all the young folks congregate to compare their vehicles and drive up and down the street for all their friends to see. And it is the street where most of the fast food places are, so most of the citizens of the old town have reason to go there too. It's really a busy place on Friday and Saturday nights."

As he drove past the Dairy Queen and Burger King, he laughed and said, "This is what we call the Royal block. The King and the Queen are side by side, and here on the other side is the Chrysler dealer." He slowed down, and as they drove past the used car lot, Roy said, "Whoa! There's a good looking van."

Herman pulled over to the curb and stopped. "You want to look 'er over, Roy?" he asked.

Roy opened the door and stepped across the curb and entered the lot between two well-polished used cars.

The used car manager, watching from his little office up the hill and to Roy's left, heaved his bulk up out of his comfortable swivel chair and came to meet Roy. As he walked toward Roy's youthful figure, he noted Roy's bare head, the muddy colored, but clean, tan tee shirt, the well washed jeans, the ill fitting sneakers. He thought, here's a poor farm kid, wants a car, and don't have any money.

Roy was walking toward the van which was five cars down the line. When he reached the van, he turned to meet the salesman.

He was a size extra large, gone to overweight, balding man about fifty years old in a white shirt, a bright orange necktie, gray pants, and a belt that cut deeply into his ample middle.

"Howdy, young man! What can I do for you?"

By this time he was much closer to Roy and had begun to revise his first impression. Condescension would not be the proper approach. "That's a nice, full size Dodge Van, sir," he said. "Low miles."

Roy opened the sliding door on the passenger side and looked in without saying anything. Empty cargo space. Roy still did not say anything, just looked. Looked new.

The salesman continued, "It was ordered just like that, a full size van with carpeted deck and sidewalls but no seats. We can install the other seats if you want 'em. It was ordered by a furniture store to use for deliveries, but they couldn't get some of the larger pieces through the doors, so they traded it in for a ton truck with a box bed. That works a lot better for them, and now we have a nice van with only a little over ten thousand miles and almost all of the warranty still on it."

Roy spoke for the first time, "Have you had any offers?"

The salesman sputtered, taken aback by the question. "Well, no. But----but we've got it priced very reasonable." He quoted a price that was even lower than Roy expected.

Roy looked in the driver's door and released the hood, then raised the hood. It was an engine that Roy was familiar with, as he was with most engines. He knew it to be a sturdy reliable engine. He would not win any drag races, but there would be plenty of power for normal driving and good fuel economy.

When he turned to leave, the salesman said, "I'll try to help you get a loan on it." He handed Roy his business card. "Mr. Snyder down at the bank is a friend of mine, and this really is a good, clean, solid van."

Roy said, "Thank you, sir." He looked at the card, "Mr. Al Fox, Mgr," he read. "I may be back in the morning." He added. "If the van is still here we can talk about it."

He put the card in his pocket as he hurried back to the car where Herman, Tildy and Linda were waiting.

When he got into the car he reached over the back of his seat to take Linda's hand. He said, "Linda, I think we should buy that van."

Linda reached for and held his hand and said, "Whatever you think, Roy. We will need some kind of transportation; it looked nice." She was leaning back against her seat wearily.

Roy said, "We still have two hours or more before Herman and Tildy have to be at the Walmart parking lot. Do you want to go to Walmart to buy some clothes?"

"Roy, honey, I don't know. I don't have any money, or credit cards, or even any identity, and I'm so tired."

Roy said, "Linda, dear, please don't worry about the money. I will take care of that."

Tildy said, "I'll help you Linda if you would want me to. They have the large carts with seats on them. You can ride and I'll push you to the various departments and you can choose the article you want and ride to the next department."

Linda said, "Oh, Tildy! You folks are so nice to us, and I feel so useless. I've never in my life felt like this before."

Tildy felt her forehead, "Well, you don't have fever. You'll feel better tomorrow, after you've rested. Do you want to try it?"

Linda smiled wanly and said, "I can't refuse the opportunity to get new clothes."

Herman said as he pulled into the parking lot, "I'll drive up to the entrance and let you all out. Then I'll park and wait by the door."

Roy said, "I'll get the cart and bring it out to the car."

As tired as he was, as soon as the car rolled to a stop at the entrance, Roy jumped out and hurried into the store. He was back in less than a minute with the cart.

Linda and Tildy got out of the car as soon as Roy appeared and Linda was soon seated comfortably. Roy pushed her into the store.

Tildy said, "I'll take you wherever you want to go, Linda."

Roy said, "First of all, let's both get a suitcase; then you go your way and I'll go mine." They headed for the luggage department. They very quickly agreed on a light blue, three piece matched set. There was a small box type case with a tray for cosmetics, toiletries, and jewelry, a medium sized conventional suitcase, and a large suitcase.

Roy grabbed the medium suitcase and put it in his cart, and he put the jewelry case and the large suitcase in Linda's cart. Then he bent over and gave her a quick kiss on the lips and said, "Are you doing all right?"

With a slight blush and a little smile, Linda said, "Yes, honey, I'll be O. K. We won't be long."

Tildy looked on approvingly.

"I'll meet you at the checkout," he said, as he started toward the Men's Wear sign.

In a few minutes he had selected a package of three briefs, size thirty-two, and package of three white vee neck tee shirts, size forty-two. He found two semi-dress, short-sleeved shirts both in light colors, with snaps instead of buttons, one blue and white with thin gray and red lines running through it and the other was a multi colored check. He tried both of them on over his muddy, tan tee shirt. They both fit. He could always wear off the rack.

He soon found jeans in his size and tried them on, one dark blue denim and two light blue. They fit. Socks! He almost forgot socks. He went back and found a package of five pairs that he could wear with his Tony Lama's.

He didn't like any of the boots so he chose a good pair of sneakers. He found a red baseball cap with the logo of his favorite team. Then he picked up a toothbrush, toothpaste, deodorant and some after-shave.

"That's it," he said to himself. "That should take care of--- Oops! I won't need after shave unless I have a razor or an electric shaver."

He grabbed a package of three safety razors off a hook just above the after-shave display. Then he pushed his basket around the end of the aisle and there was an assortment of electric shavers. He immediately saw one exactly like the shaver that was now under about twelve feet of muddy river water in his submerged pickup. That was the one he put in his basket.

He headed for the checkout lanes. As he started to cross one of the large passageways, he saw Linda and Tildy far down the aisle apparently discussing some item that Linda was holding. He went toward them. As he got closer, he could see it was a pair of white pants.

Linda was saying, "I think they'll fit but they are pretty expensive."

Roy walked up at that moment and gently took the white pants from her and laid them in the basket.

He said, "I like white pants, we'll take 'em."

"But, Roy, I already have three pairs of pants in the basket."

"Do you like them?" he asked.

"Yes, but, they are---"

"No problem," he interrupted her. "What else do you want to get?"

Tildy spoke, "I've been trying to persuade her to get one more blouse, over here. I'll show you." She led the way to a rack of blouses. One hanging on the outside caught Roy's eye immediately, a white, short sleeved cotton blouse, with beautiful stitching all around the collar and pink stitching around the sleeves, Tildy said, in a watermelon color.

Roy picked it up and asked Tildy, "Is this the one?" Tildy smiled broadly and said, "Yes, that's it." Roy turned to Linda and asked, "Does it fit? Do you like it?"

Linda said, "Yes, I like it and it's the right size but I haven't tried it on."

Roy laid it on top of the white pants.

Linda protested, "Roy, you didn't even look at the price tag."

Roy gave her that disarming grin that she couldn't resist and said, "Linda, honey, maybe we'll check price tags next week but today we're on a roll. Let's check out here and go to the motel so you can get some rest."

At the checkout Roy paid cash for everything and had a little over a hundred dollars left.

Linda said, "Thanks, Roy, you're so sweet. I can't offer to help pay. But I will when we get everything straightened out. I'm sorry, Roy." She had tears in her eyes.

When Roy saw the tears he stopped the cart and gathered her in his arms and said "Linda, Linda, please don't think this way. What's mine is ours from now on."

Roy took her face in his hands and kissed her forehead and then her lips. "Please don't think this way anymore. Just smile, and lets go try on some of these new threads." He smiled and said, "O.K.?"

Tildy patted Linda on the shoulder and said, "That's a good idea, Linda, and you both need rest."

When they got to the exit. Herman pulled the car up to the door. He popped the trunk open and they piled their purchases in and closed the lid.

In less than five minutes they were at the motel.

Herman parked under the canopy at the office and Roy went in and signed the credit card slip and picked up the two room keys

Herman drove down the row of parking spaces, most of them occupied, and backed in to number 17.

Roy got out and unlocked number 17 and 18.

Tildy helped Linda into room 17 while Herman and Roy unloaded their packages. They carried them all into number 18 and Roy said, "We'll sort them out later."

There were double doors between the two rooms and Tildy had them unlocked and opened by the time they had finished carrying everything into the room.

Roy closed the drapes and adjusted the temperature control in both rooms.

Herman said, "We'd better get back to Walmart, Tildy. Francine could be there any time now, and Roy, I'll see you tomorrow morning about eight-o-clock."

Roy and Herman warmly shook hands, and Roy said, "Herman, you folks have treated us so good. You'll have to let us make it up to you some way, some day."

Tildy said firmly, "Just be sure you are at our house tomorrow at twelve-o-clock for a chicken dinner." And she closed the door as she went out.

It had started to rain again.

Roy took Linda in his arms and said, "Do you want the north bedroom or the south bedroom?"

Linda hugged him tightly and said, with her lips against his neck, "The same one you will be in Roy."

He kissed her tenderly and she said, "Right now I just want to take a shower and lie down. I'm so weak and tired."

Roy said, "You go ahead and shower. I'll hang these new clothes on hangers and put the small stuff on the table."

Linda picked up one small package and her Emergency Kit and went into the bathroom.

All of their merchandise was in numerous plastic bags. Roy took each bag that he knew to be clothing and one at a time he emptied them on the bed. Then he took each article and arranged it carefully on a hanger and then he hung it in the closet. He put all of Linda's things on the left and his three pairs of jeans and two shirts on the right. The small stuff he took out of the bags and set on the table.

That done, he put all of the plastic bags in the wastebasket and turned down the bed and hurried into the next room and into the shower.

Roy had always found a shower to be rejuvenating and invigorating, but as soon as the hot water hit him he realized his strength and energy were all used up. As the stinging spray hit his back and shoulders, he thought about what a day this had been and all that had happened.

Not more than ten hours ago he had been swimming for his life. Literally. If he had not grasped that submerged sapling or if it had broken off in his hand, they would have been swept away by the quickening current into the large main body of the flood. He knew he had not had enough strength and energy to fight his way back to land if they missed that spit.

He was sure Linda could not have survived another twenty minutes in the water and he knew he would have soon succumbed to the numbing cold that was already affecting his coordination

At that point Providence had taken over. Roy knew that without help the current would have carried them both far out into the water with no hope of getting back to land alive.

He was so thankful to the Almighty and so grateful to Herman and Tildy for all they had done.

As he finished his shower, he realized he had brought nothing to the bathroom to wear so he wrapped a large bath towel around his middle and went into the next room.

The only light came from the bathroom that Linda had just vacated and the room that Roy had just left.

Linda was in the bed on her right side facing the empty side of the bed. She was wearing a sheer black nightgown and had the blanket pulled up to her waist. She was sound asleep with her left hand extended toward where Roy would soon be lying. She was very beautiful.

Roy just stood there and drank in the sight for a moment then turned out the light in room seventeen and dropped the towel and quietly slid in beside her.

Her fresh, clean scent and soft beauty were overwhelming. He knew how totally exhausted she was and as much as he wanted her he decided not to wake her.

He carefully slid under the blanket and lay on his left side facing her. He could feel her warmth and he smelled the familiar sweet odor of her body and her hair.

He moved just a little closer and this time when he moved, she reached out for him in her sleep and cuddled into his arms as she had done when they were under the poncho. When she reached out to him, Roy slid his left arm under her head and rolled onto his back and with both arms pulled her soft, pliable body close. All in one motion her head was on his shoulder; her left arm automatically went across his stomach. Her left leg, naked below the shortie nightgown, was over his left leg.

Roy slowly relaxed. His left hand gently and sleepily massaged her back. He was mildly aroused but happy just to lie there with her in his arms. He was so tired.

Linda wriggled a little and moved even closer and murmured, "Roy." She moaned softly, and they both drifted into a deep sleep.

Chapter 33

Tuesday Morning, Sam's Office

Sam was eating lunch at his desk at 12:10 when the phone call came from the State Police Post.

Captain Dillon and Mathew and another accident reconstruction man, a Captain Howard, would arrive at Sam's office between 12:30 and one o'clock.

Captain Howard would be in charge and he wanted Sam and Wilford and Dusty to be there to verify the facts.

Sam found Wilford and Dusty eating lunch in the outer office.

"O.K., guys," he said, " The State Police will be here in less than an hour and they want to meet with us again to reconstruct what they think happened out there. So when you see them drive in, just come on into the office."

"No matter what they say, those two vehicles can't be moved until the water goes down. And it hasn't even started to drop yet," he added.

Dusty said, as soon as he could swallow, "O.K., Sam, we'll be watching for 'em."

Wilford could only nod in agreement and say "Umfph K," around the large bite of ham on thick sliced, home made bread. When he had chewed and swallowed and washed it down with a long drink of sweetened iced tea from his half-gallon thermos, he said, "I wonder what they'll think happened out there?"

"I think it will really be interesting to hear their opinions on this situation. There are not many known facts on which they can build a story," said Dusty.

Sitting at the corner desk, Bill Owens chided, "You guys are gonna' owe us a week's pay for doing all your work while you are out playing detective."

The crew had started calling them Clint Eastwood and Inspector Cloeseau and Sherlock Holmes.

In answer to Bill's jibe, Wilford said, "We'll pay you all double time as soon as we get our consultant fee from the state."

Bill looked out the window and said, "Get ready to do some more consulting 'cause they're driving through the gate right now."

Wilford and Dusty quickly disposed of the remains of their lunch and entered Sam's office through the side door as the three officers ducked into the main entrance out of the rain.

Mathew made the introductions all around and then turned the meeting over to Captain Howard.

Captain Howard went right to the point.

"My briefing sessions with Captain Dillon, Mathew, and the divers Bob and George, along with a discussion with two other reconstruction people, has led us to a plausible story." He continued, "This is the story we plan to release to the press within the hour. Unless you fellows would have reason to question our assumptions."

"Two county road employees, trying out a new boat, have discovered two vehicles submerged in about twelve feet of water on the south side of road Eleven about one and one half miles from the Bridgton bridge. There are no reported survivors, and no bodies have been found."

"The investigation is continuing."

He paused and then said, "That is what the media will know and report on the various radio and T.V stations. It will probably be broadcast at the one-o-clock news break."

"Now, here is what we actually know."

"The pickup is registered to a Roy Johnson, age twenty four, of Broward County in Pennsylvania. His former employer has said he was going to West Kansas to visit his parents."

"The little Ford was registered to Ms. Linda Powers, age twenty three, of Litchfield, Ohio. She supposedly had no definite destination, but maybe Colorado."

"They both left their place of employment on last Friday morning on good terms with everybody."

"There is no reason to suspect they were acquainted."

"They were both suffering the loss of a spouse in the last six months."

He paused again and took a deep breath.

"Now here's where the guesswork begins."

"We think that this was probably a random encounter under the worst possible circumstances. We simply think the broken fan belt tells the story."

"Considering the position and condition of the two vehicles, we think the Escort was probably disabled and stopped on the road with the hood up. The hood was badly bent but not much other damage, a couple of cracked windows, the doors were locked and the four way flashers were in the on position. Probably the young lady had started walking toward Bridgton to get help."

"At this point in time, we theorize, Mr. Johnson arrives on the scene. He stops his vehicle a car length or two behind the Escort and gets out of his truck, leaving the door open. Right about now the levee gives way a mile up stream from Bridgton. It will only take a minute or two for that wall of water to reach Road Eleven where the two vehicles are setting. He probably hears it before he sees it. There is nothing he can do when the water slams into him. That is probably when he lost the boot. When the body is found. It's likely we will find the other boot. As for the girl, we don't know? Both bodies will probably surface by Thursday or Friday. We will alert authorities several miles downstream to be on the lookout for the bodies. We've found no reason to suspect that there were more than two people involved."

The room was very quiet. Capt. Howard searched every face and asked, "Does this sound like a reasonable story to you fellows? Are there questions?"

Sam cleared his throat and looked at Wilford and Dusty but did not speak.

Dusty was very serious when he spoke, "I'll bet that is just the way it happened."

Wilford agreed, saying, "I can't think of anything that would explain things any better. It has been on my mind a lot since we found that pickup and that car. That poor girl. They didn't have a chance, did they?"

Captain Dillon said, "When the water hit, with enough force to bowl over the car and the pickup, it had to be over very quickly for an unprotected person standing on the road. The car being lighter must have rolled completely over and came to rest on all four wheels."

"The investigation will continue," said Captain Howard, "but as for now this small press release is all we will tell the media, until we have more hard facts. I think we can conclude this meeting until such time as we do have more information, and then we will probably need to meet again to digest the new information and coordinate our response."

"I want to thank all of you for your help and cooperation."

He shook hands with Sam and Will and Dusty and said, "Till next time boys," and went out to the Patrol car.

Chapter 34

Tuesday Morning In the Motel

Roy heard someone speak his name. Again. "Roy, Roy, are you awake?" Then soft movement next to his body.

He reacted with a quick jerk. Then he was wide-awake. Realization of the situation flooded his mind immediately. He remembered getting into the bed with Linda and being so tired he could hardly move. Then sleep.

The lovely, nearly naked Linda in his arms spoke his name again.

"Roy, are you O.K.? You must have been dreaming. You were holding me so tight."

"I was dreaming. I was swimming and time was running out on us. I'm glad you woke me because it was really getting scary. I was never going to let you go."

He squeezed her and caressed her tenderly. Her body was molded against him almost full length.

He loved this beautiful woman very much. He slowly and gently moved his right hand down her back and patted her butt softly.

She pulled her face back and looked up at him shyly, "I have to go to the bathroom first."

Roy reluctantly released her and said, "I do too," as they each rolled out of the bed.

It was then Roy noticed the bedside clock.

"Damn!" Roy said sharply. Linda quickly turned and looked at him. "What, Roy? What is the matter?"

"Linda, honey, we have to meet Herman in thirty two minutes. I am sorry. I forgot to set the clock or ask for a wake up call. I wanted us to have at least a couple of hours to be together before we had to go. I'm really sorry."

Linda was in his arms in two seconds. "It's no more your fault than mine; we were both very tired." She looked into his eyes, "Our time will come, Roy, dear, very soon, and we will have time for each other."

They kissed passionately.

Linda said, "Now we must hurry. We don't want to disappoint those two wonderful people after all they've done for us."

Roy replied, "I agree one hundred percent. But I want to go on record saying I am very disappointed. I love you, Linda."

"I love you too, Roy, and the disappointment is mutual."

They both took very short showers and made quick decisions in choosing from the new clothes they had bought last night.

Herman was not surprised to see them both emerge from the same motel door, nor were they surprised to see Herman drive into their parking spot just as they stepped out.

It was seven fifty nine when Roy kissed Linda and they stepped out and closed the door.

Linda looked very pretty in her new white cotton blouse and new jeans. She had slipped on the large flannel shirt that Tildy had washed and ironed so she was dressed almost the same as when they were in the back of the pickup three days earlier.

Roy thought, "She would look beautiful and dressed up in patched, worn out overalls."

Herman said, "Looks like you folks are ready to go. Where do you want to go first?"

"We'll need to go to a bank as soon as they open," Roy said. " My bank in Bentlyville will wire us some money as soon as I give them an account number. The bank back there is open now. It's nine o-clock in Bentlyville."

Herman said, "I called John Snyder down at First National before I left home. He always gets to the bank by seven thirty. I told him I was bringing in a friend that needed to do some early banking. He said he would be glad to let us in the side door any time we showed up."

"Oh, Herman, you folks just seem to think of everything," Linda said.

"And we certainly do appreciate it," Roy added as they were getting into the car.

In less than five minutes they were getting out of the car in the bank parking lot. Herman led the way to the side entrance.

Mr. Snyder met them at the door and Herman made the introductions. They shook hands all around, and then Mr. Snyder said, "How can I help?"

"I need to call Pennsylvania to have some money transferred to your bank." Roy said, "We're going to buy a car, and license, and insurance, and we'll need about five hundred in cash. What account number shall I tell them to send it to?"

Mr. Snyder worked his computer, and in a few seconds he handed Roy a slip of paper with a new account number. "Use that desk, Mr. Johnson," he said, pointing at the desk adjacent to his own. "The phone is open to the outside line so just dial the operator or the number and I'll start setting up your checking account. I'll get you some universal checks. You can use them until we get your personalized checks printed. If anyone questions the universal checks, tell them to call me."

Roy stepped over to the designated desk and dialed the number from memory. In a few seconds he identified himself and recited his account number, and said, "I'd like to speak with Ben please."

Almost immediately he said, "Yeah, Ben, this is Roy. I need a favor." He waited just a second and said, "Thanks, Ben---I'm in--he read the city, state, and zip code, then the bank's name and street address from the letterhead on bank stationery that was lying on the desk."

"I need some money sent to this bank and to this account number," and he read the number from the paper handed to him by Mr. Snyder. There was a short pause and he repeated the account number. Another short pause, and he said, "Make it twenty thousand, Ben, from the account we set up last month."

Three sets of eyebrows went up at the mention of twenty thousand dollars.

Roy turned to Mr. Snyder and said, "What is your fax number, Mr. Snyder?"

John Snyder responded immediately with the number he had written on a sheet of paper while Roy was talking.

Roy relayed the number, then repeated it, paused again, then said, "Yeah, Ben, I'm fine and you'll be hearing from me again real soon, I promise." There was another short pause.

"That will be great, Ben."

Roy hung up the phone and swiveled his chair around to face the other desk and said, "Thanks for the use of the phone, Mr. Snyder. The deposit is on its way."

"I'm glad you got here early, Mr. Johnson, before the fax machine gets busy. Sometime we do have delays."

As he spoke, they could hear the fax machine in the next room start humming.

In another few minutes the transaction was completed and Herman, Roy and Linda again shook hands with Mr. Snyder and crossed the parking lot to Herman's car.

Roy said, "Let's go to the car lot first."

This time Herman drove onto the lot, down to where the van was parked.

Roy got out and walked around the van checking every detail. He said, "What do you think Linda? Do you like it?"

"Yes, I like it. I think it's really nice Roy. It looks almost brand new."

The salesman approached at this time. He was still wearing the white shirt and orange necktie, but this time he had black pants.

"Well sir, I didn't recognize you. It must be the hat. You still interested in the van?"

Roy quickly replied, "I'll give you," he named a figure five hundred dollars less than the man had said he wanted the evening before. "If you can have the paperwork done real quick, I'll give you a check for the full amount right here on the spot."

The man sputtered once again. "B' Bu' But sir, I don't know you, ah, You, Your, check? I don't know you sir."

Roy said, "Call your friend, Mr. Snyder, down at the bank. My name is Roy Johnson. He will O.K. my check."

Mr. Al Fox made the call. He accepted Roy's offer and in a few minutes that transaction was completed.

"Well, Linda," Roy said, as he put his arm around her shoulders, "we each own half of a Dodge Ram van. Which half do you want?"

"I'll take the passenger side for a while, then we can trade," she laughed, "like we did on the raft when we were in the water. But we better get the poncho out because it's starting to rain again."

Herman led the way to the license office. They encountered no problems there and were soon on their way with temporary plates taped inside the back window.

The next stop was the insurance office, and again Herman's presence and prestige oiled the wheels of progress.

They stepped out of the insurance office as thunder rumbled through the town, and the rain, a little heaver now, fell steadily. They stood under the canopy that extended over the sidewalk. The time was 10:30.

Roy said, "Herman, you folks have done so much for us, it is beyond thanks. We owe you our lives and all your other kindness and looking after us------and now the invitation to a chicken dinner, it's totally overwhelming."

Linda said, "Someday, we will try to find some way to repay this kindness."

"Just bring your appetites. And I'm going to hurry out and try to help Tildy with whatever is left to do." Herman replied

"See you in about an hour," he said over his shoulder as he hurried through the rain to his car. "And forget about paying for common decency."

Chapter 35

Tuesday Noon A Chicken Dinner

Roy reached for Linda's hand and as Herman drove away, he asked, "Linda honey, how are you feeling? We need to get to the motel and get things squared away there, and by the time we get that taken care of it will be time to start out to Herman's and Tildy's. Are you up for that?"

Linda smiled wanly and said, "Yes, that is what we must do but maybe we could squeeze a cup of coffee into the plan. I'm beginning to feel weak again."

Roy quickly pulled her into his arms and said, "I completely forgot. We didn't even have breakfast. I am sorry, honey."

"I forgot too," she said. "We were so involved with the van. That was a whirlwind experience!"

Roy said, "Yeah, I know. Everything happened fast but right now let's go to the nearest fast food drive up and we'll drink coffee on the way to the motel."

They dashed through the rain to the van and then drove to the Burger King window. They ordered two cups of coffee and with their coffee in hand they went straight to the motel.

Roy backed into the slot for number eighteen and unlocked their room door. Housekeeping had not reached their rooms so they hurried in and moved everything into room eighteen. Roy locked the double doors and led Linda to the bed, and said, "You lie down for a few minutes while I go to the office and pay for the other room and tell them we will keep this one for tonight. Is that O.K.?"

"Yes, that will be fine," she said. "We don't need two rooms. One bed will always be enough for us and we can certainly share a bathroom."

Roy gathered her into his arms and kissed her tenderly. "Linda, you are so beautiful. And you are wonderful. And I love you very much but I'd better hurry. It's 10:55 and we should start right away. Tildy will be looking for us."

"That's right, Roy. We'll leave as soon as you get back."

Roy was back almost before Linda could relax. He helped her to her feet and after another embrace, they locked the motel door and hurried through the rain to get into the van. They pulled into the traffic and onto the street that would take them out of town to Herman and Tildy's a twenty-five or thirty minute drive through the soggy countryside.

The strenuous pace they had kept up all morning had left Roy nearly drained of energy. He was more tired and run down than he would admit even to himself. He was grateful for the opportunity to sit in the comfortable seat in the van and drive at a leisurely pace through the hills.

Roy could tell, Linda was still very weak.

She was quiet and pale and sat limply in her seat, her head bowed forward. The seat belt and shoulder strap were snug across her lap and chest.

Roy reached over and clasped her hand, and said. "Honey, if you can rest or sleep you go right ahead. I'll drive slow and try to miss the bumps."

Linda raised her head and gave him a sweet, sincere smile as the windshield wipers beat a steady tempo, and said, "I'm not really sleepy just so very tired and weak. I felt pretty good when I first woke up but my strength and energy are both sinking fast. I don't like feeling like this."

Roy said, "You just rest. I'll turn on the radio and maybe some music will help you rest."

The radio came on.

"…and the state police are reporting at least five drownings up and down about a fifteen mile stretch of the river. Two of the drownings were the result of motorists stranded in the floodwater and trying to reach safety by wading or swimming through the raging current. Three of the victims were stranded on the roof of a low building when the building gave away under the pressure of the flood and disintegrated beneath them."

"The authorities are alerting all flood watchers down stream from Bridgton to be on the lookout for at least two bodies that have not been accounted for. More on this story on our one o-clock news break."

"This has been Randy Harris at KMTR St. Louis. And now back to The Music You Ask For."

"That's the same guy we were listening to before that wall of water hit us," Roy said.

"I was just thinking the same thing. There were probably several drownings in a flood as big as this and it's still raining," Linda replied, over the music and the rain drumming on the roof.

Roy turned the volume down on the radio and said, "You rest now if you can, we should be there in about twenty minutes and I'll bet Tildy has outdone herself."

He reached across the console and held her limp hand reassuringly for a few seconds.

"O.K., Honey, I'll just relax," She said and let her head tilt forward again and closed her eyes.

There was very little traffic so Roy drove steadily. He had no trouble remembering the route and twice when he topped a hill he could see a large expanse of floodwater in the west.

At 11:25 he turned in to Herman and Tildy's driveway. He parked in the same spot where Tildy had parked the pickup the morning before.

Almost before the van stopped rolling, Herman came out of the door with two umbrellas, one open over his head and the other closed. He handed the closed one to Roy and walked with Linda toward the house under the other.

The rain had increased in intensity as Roy followed under the other umbrella. They entered the enclosed back porch and Tildy met them at the door.

"Come in, kids!" she said happily. "You are right on time. Come in and meet Francine."

Francine stood just behind her mother. She was on crutches and her hair was in a ponytail. She was dressed in faded blue jeans and a short sleeved white blouse. The jeans had been split to the knee on the outside of the right leg to accommodate the moon boot.

Tildy said, "These are the adventurers I told you about, Francine."

"And, Linda, you still look tired but very pretty. Come in and sit at the table with Francine while I finish up. It'll be ready in about ten minutes."

Francine proved to be every bit as hospitable as Tildy and Herman and was concerned about Linda's condition. With her medical knowledge of dehydration, hypothermia, and exposure she was sure that rest and good nutrition would have Linda back to normal in a few days.

Francine said, "But, if you don't feel better tomorrow after a good meal and a night's rest it would probably be a good idea to have a check up. Our family doctor would see you without an appointment."

Tildy spoke up, "That's right. He knows we don't call him unless we really need a doctor."

Herman and Roy had each pulled a chair back against the wall and sat facing the table which was already beginning to look overloaded. The table had been extended by at least one and maybe two extra leaves, and when Tildy carried a huge steaming platter of golden brown fried chicken and set it in the middle of the table, it looked full. Nothing was missing.

Herman said, "I'll bet you and Linda are about ready for a meal like this, aren't you, Roy?"

Roy and Linda had been watching as their hunger mounted.

And Roy replied, "I was just thinking. We both ate light last Friday night. Saturday morning we both had an Egg McMuffin and coffee. From then 'till yesterday noon it was just snack crackers and warm Pepsi and oatmeal cookies. There were nearly seventy-two hours that passed without water to drink, and we rationed the snack crackers and cookies pretty thin. So, yes, we are definitely ready and this looks wonderful."

Tildy had been listening to the conversations around the table between Francine and Linda and Herman and Roy.

She found a place on the crowded table for one more bowl. It was mashed potatoes. She said, "This is it. Come and get it."

Herman placed his chair at the end of the table and Roy drew his chair up beside Linda.

Tildy sat in the chair on Francine's right, on Herman's left and across the table from Roy.

It was a lavish feast!

Chapter 36

Roy Calls Home

As the meal progressed, there was much conversation and laughter. The mood was light and cheerful. Herman and Tildy were very happy to have Francine and Linda and Roy at their table. Their genuine hospitality had made Roy and Linda really feel at ease and relaxed.

Herman said, "Roy, I want to hear more about how you two survived in that tree. There were some really severe storms those two days and nights. Lightning, thunder, rain, wind," "And hail," Linda interjected, "The wind and hail was the worst---- that was scary. I was afraid the wind would blow the tree over and I'm glad the hail didn't last very long."

Tildy interrupted, "Roy, would you please hold that story just a few minutes. I want hear it all, but there is supposed to be an important news bulletin coming on KMTR in two minutes. It is about some more drownings at Bridgton. It could be someone we know." "Sure," Roy said with a grin. "I'll have another piece of chicken, if I can hold it."

Tildy flipped on her kitchen radio, already on the station.

Randy Harris's voice came on saying, "This is the bulletin officially released by the state police just a few minutes ago.

"Two county road employees, trying out a new boat, have discovered two vehicles submerged in about twelve feet of water on the south side of Road Eleven about one and one half miles from the Bridgton bridge.

"There are no reported survivors and no bodies have been found. The investigation is continuing."

Roy looked quickly at Linda. Her eyes were wide and her mouth was slightly open but neither of them spoke.

Randy Harris's voice continued.

"That is the official news bulletin but just a few minutes before air time I had a telephone conversation with Captain Howard at the State Police Post. He said they think they know the names of two people involved and they think there are only two but they are not releasing the names pending notification of next of kin. They think the bodies will surface somewhere downstream today or tomorrow."

"My God, Roy! That's us!" Linda exclaimed. "They think we've drowned."

Roy grabbed Linda's hand. "I've got to call Mom and Dad right now and you will have to call your aunt in Wisconsin!"

Linda said, "Call your parents first. I don't know my Aunt's number. It is in my purse in your pickup."

"Use my cell phone," Francine said, unclipping it from her belt and handing it to Roy.

Herman said to Linda, "Use the landline. The operator will help you get her number."

Roy was already dialing the cell phone.

Helen Johnson answered on the third ring.

Roy said, "Mom?"

Helen said, "Roy, where are you? We've been worried about you! Are you all right?"

Her voice was full of motherly concern.

Roy started to speak when he heard a click from the other end. "Dad, are you on the other phone?" He wanted them both on the line when he told them about Linda.

His father answered, "Yeah, son, Hank needs to talk to you. If you left Friday morning, you should have been here sometime Sunday."

"Well, Dad, Mom, I'll have to tell you all about it later but I was delayed a little by a flood."

Tildy smiled at the under statement.

Roy continued, "And by a beautiful woman."

Helen spoke sharply in contrast to Joe's easygoing manner. "Roy, stop teasing. We have really been worried about you since Hank called Monday morning."

"I'm sorry, Mom, but I'm not teasing. I do have a beautiful woman that you will see just as soon as we can get there, and if the arrangements can be made we would like to get married sometime in the next two weeks right there in Goodland. Call Ellie and tell her to plan to be home next weekend."

Linda had heard the phone ring several times at her aunt's house with no answer so she hung up in time to hear Roy's last statement. She blushed and came quickly to his side.

Roy put his arm around her shoulders and drew her close. He kissed her cheek as he listened to his Mother saying, "Roy, you must be teasing. We didn't even know you were dating anyone."

"I haven't been dating anyone, Mom. Linda and I met just last Saturday and we haven't been apart since and we don't want to ever be apart."

Linda smiled and nodded approvingly with her head on Roy's shoulder.

"Mom and Dad, you both deserve a lot more explanation than I can give you over the phone but please don't judge this story good or bad until we get there, until you meet Linda and hear the whole story."

"Well, Son, you've always been on the level with us so we won't have any trouble with your story, but now I'm anxious to meet your Linda," Joe said.

Helen said, "Well, I am anxious too, Roy. She must be a wonderful person but this is certainly a big surprise, and I want to meet Linda too, so do hurry home."

"I will hurry but there are some details we'll have to attend to before we can start," Roy said. "I'll explain that later too. So bye for now. We'll see you soon."

Helen and Joe both said good-bye, and they all hung up.

Roy said, "Now I think we had better call the police and then call Hank."

Herman said, "Roy, when you get the police on the line ask for Captain Howard. He is a friend Willie went to school with years ago. He was here at our house a lot when they were in school. We've always stayed in touch and he knows where we live; maybe I can help him believe what you will tell him. Here is his number." He handed Roy a card.

"That will probably simplify things a lot," Roy said.

Chapter 37

Contact The State Police

When Roy got the State Police on the line, he asked to speak with Captain Howard. In a few seconds Captain Howard came on.

"Captain Howard here."

Roy said, "Sir, I am Roy Johnson and here with me is Linda Powers. I believe you think we drowned when our vehicles were swept off the road in the flood."

Roy could hear the sharp intake of breath when he mentioned their names.

In a controlled voice Captain Howard asked, "Where are you now?"

Roy answered, "We are in the home of Herman and Tildy Schultze."

"Herman and Tildy, are they all right? Let me talk to Herman!" The captain demanded excitedly.

Roy handed the phone to Herman. "He wants to talk to you."

"Herman! Are you all right! Is everything O.K.?" he asked sharply.

Herman answered in his slow easy drawl.

"Sure, Eddie, everything's fine. Tildy just fixed a big fried chicken dinner for our guests and there's three, no four pieces left. Why don't you come out and have a piece of cold chicken.

Come out and meet our guests and hear their story. Francine is here too and she'll be glad to see you."

"I certainly do need to talk to those folks" he said quickly. "This puts a whole new light on this news story.

"Put Mr. Johnson on again."

When Roy got on again, he asked, "Can you stay there at Herman's house for awhile? I need to get yours and Miss Powers' statements. I can be there in thirty minutes."

Roy said, "Yes, we can stay and we'll have some questions for you too."

Chapter 38

The State Police Are Astonished

True to his word, Captain Howard was there in just over thirty minutes with Captain Dillon. They parked the police car behind Roy's van and hurried in through the rain.

Captain Howard introduced Captain Dillon to Herman and Tildy and Francine and then Herman introduced both officers to Roy and Linda.

Captain Dillon said, "We sure didn't expect to find you two young people alive. How did you survive that wall of water that knocked your vehicles over?"

"How did you get here? How long have you been here?"

Those questions and more came from the two officers as quick as they could ask them until Herman interrupted them with a grin, saying, "Hold on, Eddie. Let them tell it from the beginning."

Roy moved his chair just a little closer to Linda and put his arm over her shoulders protectively. Linda moved comfortably toward him as he started to speak.

"We'll tell you the high spots. It would take three days to tell all that happened since we met."

"You mean you didn't know each other before?" Captain Dillon asked incredulously!

"That's right," Roy said, and Linda nodded her head.

"We will explain it all as we go"

"You boys won't go to sleep while they tell this story," Herman said with a wide grin.

Linda started by telling how Roy fixed the leaking valve on her tire at the gas station and how reluctant she was to drive on when she saw that immense expanse of water, and the road looked so small from the top of that hill and so empty. And her car started slowing down and acting strange before she was half way through that long stretch. And then it stopped!

Roy spoke, "I saw the car as I came down the hill. I figured someone must be having trouble and I have always stopped to see if I could help in a case like that."

"I was so glad to see him," Linda said, and leaned closer to Roy

The story wound on to where the wall of water hit them and rolled the lighter Escort over and scooted the pickup across the blacktop. The Escort was immediately submerged.

"We were in the back of the truck but the water kept rising so we put the cooler on top of the cab and sat on it in the rain," Roy said. "It gave us time to form a plan."

Linda looked proudly at Roy. "It was a very good plan," she said.

"When the pickup finally went over," Roy continued, "we held on to the handles of the cooler to keep us afloat and just rode the current."

They kept their narrative in sequence through the tree, the stormy nights, the long swim to shore, and the timely rescue by Herman and Tildy, up to the call to Captain Howard.

There were many interruptions and questions and at one point Captain Howard said, "I'd like to see that cooler."

Herman said, "It's right out here on the porch," and everyone but Tildy trekked out to the enclosed back porch to look at the cooler.

Captain Howard opened the cooler and saw the empty Pepsi bottles, and the wrappers for the snack crackers, the empty oatmeal cookie bag and the poncho.

Capt. Howard said, "You had to be very resourceful to come through all you've been through the last three days."

"And very lucky," Roy said, squeezing Linda a little with his arm over her shoulders. "Linda was wonderful through it all. She never panicked or complained. We just did what we thought we had to do to get back to civilization."

"Roy was very resourceful," Linda said. "His ideas were always the best option and we were determined to survive and to be together."

After nearly four hours of telling the story and answering questions Roy said, "I guess that's our story and now we have a couple of questions. Like, when and what will become of our vehicles?"

Captain Howard took the question. "It will be three or four weeks before the water goes down enough to hook on and winch them back onto the road. And when it does go down we may find some heavy damage on the road that would have to be repaired before we could get to them. But when we can, they will be towed to the State Police post and stored on our back lot until you folks can sort through the stuff for anything that will be salvageable. We will arrange to have a dumpster there for the things that are completely ruined."

Linda and Roy were both nodding approval and Linda said, "That will work out good for us." Roy added, "Notify us when that time comes."

Captain Dillon, with a slight tone of alarm in his voice said, "Eddie, do you know it's after five thirty? We've been here all afternoon."

With a grin Captain Howard said, "I know. We must go. But this story was worth every minute we spent here."

Tildy emerged from the kitchen. "Hold on, Eddie. You can't go yet. Francine and I have fixed up a snack for you all and it's almost supper time. Come on in to the kitchen."

"I know your snacks, Tildy, so headquarters will just have to wait a little longer," Eddie said, grinning and rubbing his stomach.

Roy said, "Actually, we meant to get started early in the afternoon to rest and get an early start tomorrow. My folks are anxious to meet Linda. But maybe we'll just have to start a little later. Tildy's and Herman's hospitality is irresistible."

It was an elaborate snack. Tildy had added yet another leaf to the table and at each place was a large slice of watermelon. There was homemade bread, three different kinds of cold cuts, a cheese plate, and fresh sliced peaches. There was coffee and tea and various flavors of soda to drink. Pickles, olives, relish and more.

Captain Dillon said, "This is far too much to be called a snack."

The two officers, not having had the pleasure of the big chicken dinner, dived in with gusto.

Roy and Linda had eaten heartily at noon and at five forty five they were not very hungry. They ate the watermelon and a little of the other fruit. Roy had a small sandwich and they both had coffee.

The conversation was light and occasionally one of the officers would ask Roy or Linda about their harrowing experience or the contents of their vehicles.

A little after six, Eddie Howard said, "We really do have to get back to headquarters but the time we have spent here today has certainly been worth while and it has been a real pleasure to meet the two of you. All of the officers at the police post are amazed that you were able to survive that wall of water that bowled your vehicles over, and the boys at the county road office will be very surprised and happy to learn that you are both alive and well."

He stood up and shook hands with Roy and Linda and he gave Francine and Tildy a hug. And he said to Roy and Linda, "Keep in touch with us and as soon as we can get to your vehicles we will tow them out."

Roy replied " That will be fine. " and the two officers went out to the squad car.

Chapter 39

The End And The Beginning

When they had gone, Roy looked at Linda and their eyes met in complete understanding and approval. He then turned to Herman and Tildy and said, "We really should go too. We need to get a couple of cell phones before we start out for Kansas tomorrow morning."

Tildy had noticed they had been holding hands and now Roy put his arm around Linda. She leaned willingly toward him with a warm smile, as Roy asked, "Do you think any electronic shop would be open as late as seven o-clock where we might be able to buy cell phones yet today?"

Francine answered, "I think that electronics store that is two blocks east of Walmart stays open as late as Walmart. They sell three or four different brands of cell phones including Trac phones."

"That sounds good to me," Roy said, "and I forgot to get a toothbrush last night so that will be another stop before we start packing those suitcases."

Linda said, "I want to get your phone numbers and your mailing addresses so we can keep in touch. We'll be going a lot of miles from here but we will always be together and we can never, ever, forget your kindness and your hospitality."

"That's right," Roy added. "You saved our lives and that is something we can never forget. We will always owe you."

Herman spoke, "Now you kids just forget about owing anybody, anything. We are just glad that we were able to help. We enjoyed your company and wish you could stay longer." Tildy added, "You must come back soon and show us pictures of the wedding."

Francine handed Linda a small note pad with their phone numbers and addresses that she had written during the conversation. She gave Linda a hug. Then Tildy and Herman each gave Linda hugs. Herman and Roy warmly shook hands and both Tildy and Francine gave Roy a hug.

Linda and Roy both started to talk at the same time. Roy stopped to let Linda talk first.

She said, "Tildy, that was a wonderful meal you had for us. I know it was a lot of work and everything was delicious."

Roy said, "That is exactly what I was going to say. But Linda said it better. You really went overboard." As they walked through the door onto the enclosed back porch, Herman said, "I'll bring your cooler out to the van, Roy. You can take Linda out with the umbrella and I'll bring the umbrella back."

Linda said, "You folks are just so nice. You think of everything and you couldn't have made us feel more welcome."

When they got to the van, Roy got Linda in her seat and turned and gave the umbrella to Herman. They shook hands again, firmly, and Roy said, huskily, "I hope to see you folks again, real soon."

With that, Roy hurried through the light rain around to the driver's seat.

Herman was still standing by the van door, under the umbrella. Tildy and Francine were standing in the doorway waving, and as Roy started the engine, Herman reached up and patted Linda's arm and said, "You kids hurry back."

They pulled out of the driveway and onto the road.

Linda said, "Those are the nicest people I have ever met."

Roy said, "Me too."

They were quiet for a while as Roy drove along the wet country roads, each lost in their own thoughts of their ordeal, their ultimate rescue, and the overwhelming hospitality of Herman and Tildy. Finally Roy said, "We have a couple of stops to make. Can you think of anything we need to take with us on the road?"

Linda looked at Roy apologetically, "I'm still wearing Francine's shoes. I would like to get a pair of low heel, white shoes. I know they have them at Walmart. They don't cost very much."

Roy looked quickly at her and put his foot on the brake and pulled to the side of the road and stopped! He reached over the console and took her hand.

"Linda, Honey, I love you! I don't care how much they cost. We'll get the best pair of shoes they have, O. K?"

She looked at him with tears in her eyes and said, "I love you too, Roy, but you have already bought me so many nice things."

"That's just the start, Honey. I'm going to be giving you things the rest of your life."

He released her hand and put the gear selector in drive and said, "We are almost to town. We'll stop first at the electronics store and get a couple of cell phones. Then we'll head to Walmart for shoes and a toothbrush and toothpaste and whatever else we might see that we need and then go to our room at the motel!"

Linda said tremulously, "Roy, I love you very much," and reached for his hand.

The stop at the electronics store was easy. They bought his and her phones, a brand they were both familiar with and left with both A.C. and vehicle chargers.

Just two blocks down the street to Walmart, they parked close and hurried in through the light rain.

Holding hands, they went directly to the shoe department.

Linda found the type and color and size shoes she was looking for immediately and then they went to the pharmacy and selected a toothbrush and tooth paste and then to the checkout, all in a matter of minutes.

They suddenly realized they were in a hurry and when they got to the van, Roy opened the door and grabbed Linda and standing in the light rain, they enjoyed a long, passionate kiss.

Some guy in the next row, just getting out of his car, gave out with a long, low wolf whistle.

They just looked at him and grinned and then jumped into the van and drove on out to the motel.

As soon as they got into the room, they joined in another passionate embrace, and Roy said, "Linda, when we were in the water, I asked if you would marry me. You said yes! Is that still your answer?"

"My answer was yes, Roy Dear, a thousand times yes!"

They were locked in each other's arms.

Roy said,. "Linda, Honey, a honeymoon was mentioned a little while before my proposal. "Do you think we could start our honeymoon just a little early?"

Linda said, "I will be very disappointed if we don't."

Together they walked to the door, and Roy hung out the sign that said:

ᴅO ᴎOT ᴅISTUᴙᴃ!